BENARES
and
IN BABYLON

Barlen Pyamootoo

Translated from the French by Will Hobson

CANONGATE

First published in English in Great Britain in 2004 by
Canongate Books Ltd, 14 High Street,
Edinburgh EH1 1TE

Originally published individually in French as *Benares*
and *Le tour de Babylone* in 1999 and 2002 respectively
by Éditions de l'Olivier, le Seuil

10 9 8 7 6 5 4 3 2 1

The publisher acknowledges subsidy from the Scottish Arts Council
towards the publication of this volume.
This book is supported by the French Ministry for Foreign Affairs,
as part of the Burgess programme headed for the French Embassy
in London by the Institut Français du Royaume-Uni.

Liberté • Égalité • Fraternité
RÉPUBLIQUE FRANÇAISE

British Library Cataloguing-in-Publication Data
A catalogue record for this book is available on
request from the British Library

ISBN 1 84195 337 7

Typeset in 11.5/17pt Goudy (Old Style) by
Palimpsest Book Production Limited,
Polmont, Stirlingshire
Printed and bound by
Nørhaven Paperback A/S, Denmark
Book design by James Hutcheson

www.canongate.net

BENARES

One day Mayi came over to my place. I was living opposite the store; I hadn't been there long. It was only a one-room house, but it had a yard that made it bigger when you opened the door and the window, and there was a spreading tree in the middle of the yard that blocked out the sky and the sun and gave shade all day long, which was good when it got hot. Alongside the yard ran a dirt track, which was used by lovers and people going off to smoke a joint or coming back from doing so, it led to the sea and a vast beach that offered plenty of privacy. The track was also used by men who liked to drink but they didn't go anywhere, they just stayed glued to the store and that was a long way from the sea. Further still were the clinic, the post office and the houses, some of which had stood empty for a long time; after those came a huge sugar-cane field, which seemed to cut the village in half, and then, in single file, the school, my parents' house and Mayi's house.

It was getting light when I saw Mayi. He was walking

alongside the cane field, dragging his feet and looking at the ground; he seemed to be thinking about something deep, important. I thought about his job as soon as I saw him; I'd just shaved and I was getting dressed to go to work. If we were joking around, we'd say that he was a second-division fisherman: he didn't fish out past the lagoon because he couldn't handle the swell out there. When he reached the post office he stopped and turned around. The sun kept on rising and getting bigger while the road sliced through the whole village like a painted set, silent and motionless and somehow deep as well: it looked as if it had foundered, sunk.

Mayi took a handkerchief out of his pocket and meticulously wiped his face as if he were removing make-up in front of a mirror, caressing himself; he made it seem as if he was looking at himself as he did so. Then he set off again, keeping out of the sun. Now and then he'd stop abruptly or slow down and say something to people I couldn't see but could imagine leaning their elbows on their windowsills or sitting on their doorsteps. The road wound downwards, with small wood and corrugated-iron houses lining it on either side. I moved away from the window as Mayi passed the clinic and sat on the bed to put on my trousers. By the time I stood up he'd already pushed open the door. He stopped on the doorstep for a moment, his face raised towards the ceiling. He seemed to be studying its texture; he looked so serious, so studious. Then he came towards me, his eyes sleepy, slightly lost, and asked me for a cigarette. He took a very long drag and tilted his head back to exhale, through his nose and his mouth, and that lasted a long time. It was strange how his eyes lit up his face as he exhaled and the smoke rose to the ceiling. When there was no more smoke to exhale, he put out the cigarette and started coughing. He slipped two fingers into his shorts' pocket, took out a dirty, crumpled handkerchief and wiped his nose, his mouth and his whole face. Then he broke into a smile that made him even more handsome: yesterday he'd won two thousand rupees at cards and he wanted us to go and find a woman each to bring back for the night.

I came home from work at about five. Mayi was waiting for me. He was leaning against my front door, smoking. It was nerves, he said so himself as he stubbed out his cigarette. He'd dressed up; it was the first time I'd seen him in a shirt and a pair of trousers: he'd always worn shorts and a football shirt for as long as I'd known him. They made him look older, more important. I reminded him tersely that the taxi wouldn't be there til six. It wasn't that he was annoying me, but I was tense and tired and I felt like being on my own for a while, long enough to forget about work. Mayi looked off towards the store and murmured something, of which I only caught the word 'sure', and then he looked back at me and shrugged his shoulders, 'That's all.' Then he went home; he said he'd be back at six. I had a shower and washed my hair. I put on a pair of jeans and a t-shirt with 'Miami' written on it. I like clothes which have something to read on them; that's what I read the most.

Mayi and Jimi arrived at the same time. Whenever I was bringing a woman back for the night, I always took Jimi as the driver. I liked his manners a lot – for instance, the way, when he spoke to people, he only talked about what mattered. We set off straightaway. I sat next to Jimi; Mayi was in the back, directly behind me. He didn't say anything – maybe it made him shy going on a trip like that, it was his first time. I turned round every now and then; I wanted to check that everything was ok, that he wasn't bored. Each time he'd be gazing up at the sky and he'd seem very moved.

We got to Port-Louis just before seven. We drove round the whole town, practically street by street, and went to the docks, not just once but several times, but all we saw were men. It was too early. So Jimi suggested taking us to Pointe aux Sables. He said that there were women standing on every street corner over there and that he'd never seen the likes of it anywhere else, so many women all in one place. 'You can take your pick and then we'll be off home.' We drove round the village five times, and it was only on the last circuit that we actually even saw a woman. She was at a bus stop with a man who must have been her pimp. She waved at us to stop and asked, 'Are you looking for girls?' I said we were looking for two. She told us we wouldn't have any problems there. I added that we wanted to take them home. She wanted to know where. I said Benares. That put her right off. She took a step backwards, abruptly turned round and went back to join her pimp at the bus stop. It was him who told us, 'Benares is too far. She's never even heard of it.'

'It's not as far as all that . . .' but he probably didn't hear me, since just at that moment a bus drew up between us, drowning out my voice. Two women got out. That only left the driver on board the bus and he was in a hurry. He set off up the hill at top speed, while the two women took it in turns to kiss the pimp. A long kiss each time. There was some laughing, and then they all left the bus stop. After a few steps, the pimp turned and nodded at us, encouragingly I think. I gave him a wave and watched, without regret, the women struggling to get up the hill. They looked like three barrels that might tip over at any moment and come hurtling downhill.

'So now what do we do?' asked Jimi, stealing a glance at Mayi.

Mayi didn't say anything. He continued unhurriedly biting his nails. He seemed lost in a dream; he had the sort of look in his eyes you get when you let your thoughts wander, evanescent, something like that. He must have been mulling things over. He had leaned his elbows on the door and was looking into the distance. He seemed almost to be rising up through the car roof into the sky, perhaps because the road fell at such a steep angle. The sky was a monotonous grey, the sea too, probably, along with everything else there was to see down below if he had leaned out further. But he just looked up, at the grey, monotonous sky.

Several times I thought I heard footsteps and laughter and a vague murmur that sounded like singing – but as far as I could see, in every direction the streets remained hopelessly deserted. So finally I yelled at the top of my voice, 'What the fuck are they all doing?' and I looked at my watch as if we were meant to be meeting somebody. It was late, almost eight o'clock.

'I saw a ship in harbour just now,' said Jimi. 'A big one, rust everywhere . . . Maybe it docked today.'

'What difference would that make?' I didn't understand what he was driving at.

'That'd explain why there aren't any women around,' he said, looking towards the trees that lined the other side of the street and the sky beyond them.

'They're not going to get the show on the road if there aren't any sailors around, because the sailors are the ones who'll push up the prices,' and then he turned slowly and lit a cigarette out of the wind, 'and they're not going to come cheap tonight either, because they'll be few and far between.'

'So what time's this show going to start?'

Jimi stared at his watch for a long time, he must have been counting the hours and the minutes, and then he looked up with an embarrassed smile. 'Well, not that soon. The sailors are otherwise engaged and they will be for quite a while yet.'

'Fighting?'

Jimi swung his arms like a boxer and laughed. 'Just enough to stop them getting rusty.'

'So now what do we do?' It was my turn to ask.

Mayi was still biting his nails – he'd just changed hand – and his eyes had the same look in them as before, except that now they were turned on the fields, the houses and the sea. We could see the harbour but no big ship. I almost said as much to Jimi but I realised just in time that we couldn't see the whole harbour.

Jimi answered in a noncommittal voice, 'Let's go to Ma Tante's.'

I didn't know Ma Tante but I'd often heard about her and her establishment that was closed at night because the women she employed had husbands and children who they went home to in the evenings after work. And of course the husbands knew what they did but they turned a blind eye; they were too poor to refuse the money, or too greedy. I'd also heard about the beds in the rooms having concrete bases – so they wouldn't break under the strain of all those men thrashing around, I was told. Then I thought about Ma Tante again and her establishment that she shut at night: I said to myself that it must be because she had a husband too. 'Won't we be disturbing her, though?' I asked, tugging at Jimi's arm to make him turn round. 'Her place is shut at night, isn't it?'

'It's just to help us out, give us an address,' Jimi said softly but firmly, 'and even if she can't, at least it'll pass the time until the sailors have stopped fighting each other.'

We drove back through Port-Louis. It looked like a city during wartime; there wasn't a single woman on the streets – just some dogs and a few men who seemed to be waiting for a curfew to begin, some signal for them to break up and go their separate ways. Then we took the road for Sainte Croix where we turned right after a petrol station and drove about a hundred metres along a road that was being tarred; there were signs pointing this out pretty much everywhere.

'It's like an advert,' murmured Jimi and he leaned

towards me and asked, 'Elections?' I said I had no idea but that I'd be surprised, I hadn't seen any posters saying anything about an election. 'That's what surprises me,' said Jimi, 'that there aren't any posters.' He seemed to be looking for some as he slowed down. And there were a few, but they were for films. Jimi muttered a few words I didn't understand, they seemed from a different age, and then he stopped in front of a house that was floodlit and had a garden with roses of all sorts of colours. Clearly it was for the roses that there were lights above every door and window: so as not to lose any of their colours. A path crossed the garden; it was straight and narrow and so spotless that it gleamed as brightly as the roses. I looked at the house and pictured the people who lived there and the sorts of jobs they might have. Maybe they worked in a bank or a Government department, or maybe they were in business. I thought of other, less common professions, but the main thing I thought was how right they were to like roses. 'Respectable people,' as the saying goes, and I didn't understand why Jimi had stopped in front of their house.

'Why are you stopping here?'

'This is where Ma Tante lives,' Jimi answered.

'Are you sure?' I looked at the garden and its gleaming flowers and gleaming path for a long time. Every rose displayed its halo of light like a precious stone and I could easily distinguish every slightest nuance of shade but I would have been completely incapable of putting the infinite variety of their yellows, whites and reds into words.

'This is it, right here,' said Jimi and he got out of the car. He waited to slam his door at the same time as we did. 'So we only make a noise once,' he explained.

Then we crossed the garden in silence, sweating and taking shuffling, rhythmic little steps like sleep-walkers. The heat was heavy, soporific. 'It's like being in a greenhouse,' I said to Jimi who had taken out his handkerchief. It was a funny handkerchief, of a sort I had never seen before: it was embroidered and barely broader than the palm of a hand. He mopped his face and forearms, then carefully folded it in four before putting it back in his pocket, 'Maybe that's what this is, with all these flowers and lights.' He stopped at the front door and called 'Ma Tante! Ma Tante!'

The door opened immediately and a woman who wasn't as young as she used to be appeared on the doorstep. It was Ma Tante, looking just as people had described her to me. She was very fat with a hatchet face; she had thick lips, broad shoulders, and arms and legs that jutted out like solid, sturdy beams. Her hair was black and curly and her voluminous breasts strained against a blouse that was as dark a brown as her skin. Her mouth was open, probably with delight at our visit.

I tried to work out her age but I couldn't. Her face was furrowed with wrinkles but her eyes were as bright as a young girl's. They seemed even younger when she recognised Jimi: a glint suddenly stole into them as furtive as a will-o'-the-wisp. She grabbed the hand Jimi held out to her and snuggled up to him for a long while, and then she kissed both of us, Mayi and me, and clasped us in her arms. She was very strong; I'd been told that she'd hit men if they didn't pay or were looking for trouble.

'Come in, come in,' Ma Tante said, gesturing to the door, and she led the way into a room at the back of the house. That was a terrible shock; the colours in it were such a contrast to those in the garden. The room wasn't painted and the roughcast plaster of its walls had turned the colour of mildew – a mixture of green, grey and chestnut – and what's more it smelled of cement. Luckily the window was open and a weak but steady breeze blew through the room before dashing itself against some posters on the far wall that had come half-unstuck and rustled constantly. You couldn't really make what they were of anymore – some breasts maybe, or were they buttocks? Apart from the posters, a handful of cane armchairs stood around a low table, on which there were some plastic glasses arranged in a circle, two ashtrays, an old magazine, some brochures for a hotel in Rodrigues and, in the middle, a cracked mirror. Before sitting down, Jimi took a flask of rum out of one of his trouser pockets and up-turned four of the glasses. But Ma Tante told him she didn't drink anymore except on Sundays on account of the fact she had a galloping heart. Jimi filled a glass for her anyway – 'That's for Sunday' – and put the flask back in his pocket. He gave her the latest news from Benares and told her about the men she didn't see anymore 'because they haven't got time these days', he explained, 'or if they do, it's already evening and then it's too late.' He told her about things that had changed, about his job and the hotel where he did fill-in work, about the tourists who spent their holidays there – Germans, French, Italians and people from other countries as well, but not so many of them – and he said how strange it felt being surrounded by all those whites who spoke so kindly to him; he'd never come across that before, people who asked so many questions. 'It's strange,' he murmured, and he wiped his forehead pensively with his handkerchief, 'it's like being on another planet . . .' After a silence that seemed long and heavy to me, he told Ma Tante that we were looking for two women to take home. Then he added, 'And tomorrow, first thing, I'll see them back to their place.'

'Why don't you go to Maman's?' Ma Tante said with a sigh, looking idly round at the posters, the floor, the glasses and the empty armchairs.

Maman lived at the end of the street; Jimi took the car and Mayi and I walked. All along the road there were people taking the air and chatting, sitting on benches or chairs; they stopped talking when we got close to them and stared at us unselfconsciously, like night birds.

Mayi paid them no mind; he walked along, looking up most of the time at the pigeons cooing on the rooftops or the trees that cast shadows on his face and seemed like shadows themselves in the sky. The street climbed, bent to the right and then fell, bulging slightly, towards a plain dotted with houses. At the point where it became narrow and winding, a path led off it which was equally meandering and lined with brambles and bushes. After taking a look behind me, I ran off down it; I told Mayi that I wouldn't be long and I tried to pee quickly, leaning on a bush. Plastic bags swirled above my head. Some, probably the same ones, caught on the electric wires or blew free every time the wind got up. I thought they were as beautiful as a bird in flight, as unnerving, and I said so to Mayi when I rejoined him. He didn't respond. He was looking vaguely at the twists and turns of the path with a vexed expression on his face and I wondered if he'd heard me; he seemed so far away from me, so far away from where we were – it must have been because he didn't feel good about being there. I put my hand on his shoulder and said casually, 'You're not saying very much . . . Is anything wrong?'

'No, no,' he answered, smiling, his voice soft and lazy. 'I've never felt as good as this.' And as if to prove it, he buried his hands in his trouser pockets, took a few steps on tiptoe – it looked as if he were floating on air – nimbly pirouetted on his heels and turned back to face me. He stopped dead in the middle of the road, his face raised towards the sky, 'Do you think it's going to rain?'

'Oh no,' I answered – the clouds seemed harmless to me, so far off in the sky. 'Not for the time being anyway.'

'How about the women?' he asked and he looked furtively in every direction as if he wanted to avoid meeting my eyes. Then he shut his eyes and bowed his head and I thought for a moment that he was going to fall asleep. When he opened them again, he looked as if he had woken up from a terrible nightmare; his whole face was sheet white, his lips were working without producing a sound and his eyes were rolling and blinking like a wanted man's. 'I thought it was easier,' and he smiled at me without parting his lips which kept on working.

'What if I gave him a shake?' I was thinking, because it got on my nerves seeing him so worked up over such a little thing. I took his face in my hands and forced him to look at me, but when I saw something that looked like sadness in his eyes, I let my hands slide down to his shoulders and said in a soft, almost sing-song voice, 'There's no need to worry, we'll soon find a couple . . . We've got the money, that's the main thing.'

'That's true,' and he patted his trouser pockets, his money. Then suddenly he grabbed his penis and stroked it, slowly sliding his hand up the shaft. 'Sailors aren't the only ones with one of these.' He said it again, laughing, as he smoothed out the creases in his trousers. His whole body was quivering, shaken by periodic little tremors that seemed to keep him steady, like a balancing pole.

Somewhere on the plain a car engine roared dully and a dog barked; then other cars and other dogs joined in. It sounded like a manhunt; there was something ferocious and furious about the barking. Shadows raced across the fronts of houses and fences, chasing headlights' flying beams. We started walking again when the commotion died down. The shadows scattered and returned to their shelters, heads down, sniffing the ground and whimpering.

'It's Jimi,' Mayi said after we'd gone a few steps. 'I find it hard talking in front of him.' He gave a plastic bottle lying in the road a big kick, then an empty tin can another, 'If you knew how uncomfortable it makes me feel . . .'

I wondered how he'd got round to Jimi. Out loud I said, 'Why's that?'

'Because he's like my grandfather,' answered Mayi. 'I mean he could be, he's old enough.' He held up his head and stuck out his chest and stared at me, horrified, 'I mean, can you imagine you and your grandfather going on a trip like this together?'

'Why not?' I said, 'It could be funny.'

'Well, that's why I haven't been saying anything.'

'Jimi isn't your grandfather,' I said. 'He's a friend. And he's not as old as you think, he's even a bit of a child sometimes,' and I put my hand on his shoulder again. 'When he tells a story, for instance, have you noticed, he always starts . . .'

'Yes, yes,' he answered, nodding his head carelessly, 'I've noticed that too,' and he started kicking the stuff in the road again: bottles, bits of cloth, tin cans, cardboard boxes, broken or chipped plates that had once been of some use. 'It still doesn't stop me feeling uncomfortable . . . Do you understand?'

We walked arm in arm along a canal that smelled of rancid oil and stagnant water, and then we crossed a bridge at the same time as some dogs, although they did so at a run. They joined another group of dogs who were waiting for them on the other bank and who looked as if they'd been running as well, their tongues were hanging out and their muzzles were covered with foam. They had to tally up the points amongst themselves, and then suddenly they all ran off through the tall grass towards a church. It must have been a stage race. Jimi was watching them as well. He was leaning against the car and drumming his fingers on the bonnet in time with their racing legs, as if he were playing an instrument. I wanted to surprise him, give him a fright so he'd jump like a child and let out a scream, but he heard the leaves crackling under our feet. He turned round; in the distance a church bell rang and, as soon as he saw us, he looked at his watch, 'Already nine.'

A few little taps on the door and a woman who looked strangely like Ma Tante opened a window and leaned her elbows on the sill. The same hatchet face, the same full-lipped mouth, the same cheerful look in her eyes, discreet and faintly surprised. I immediately thought of twins and I'm sure Mayi did as well; he seemed just as taken aback as me when the woman had leaned out of the window.

'Maman?' Jimi asked hesitantly. She nodded in a knowing way. Then Jimi went up to the window, raised himself on tiptoe and whispered something in Maman's ear along the lines of 'Ma Tante sent us'. She waved at him to wait and shut the window again. Then she opened the door and led the way into a room that also looked strangely like Ma Tante's. It wasn't painted either and smelled just as strongly of cement. But it's true that, instead of erotic posters, there were three pictures of gods hanging in a row on one wall.

'That's lucky,' said Maman, 'I just happen to have two who don't know where to sleep tonight.' As she was talking, she turned slightly and, looking at the wall, with the pictures of the gods on it, she called out in that direction, 'Ladies!'

We heard banging, then approaching footsteps. Two women entered the room and crossed it as if they were on parade. They walked slowly and resolutely, without looking at us, their arms at their sides, perhaps so as to allow us every chance to admire them. When they got to the end of the room, they spun around as smartly as a soldier doing an about-face. Then they leaned against the wall and with a cheerful, mischievous

air, as though they had nothing to do with the proceed-
ings, acknowledged us with a few sighs and a slight nod
of the head. Jimi tried to persuade them, but they didn't
want to have a drink or to sit down. The one with a
lovely smile was called Zelda; Mina, on the other hand,
looked sad, if anything, when she smiled. Maybe she
had a temperature: she was wearing a jumper and
trousers and she seemed exhausted. There were rings
beneath her eyes, pale but still deep, and a criss-cross
of little lines at the corners of her mouth that made her
smile melancholic, close to tears.

Zelda seemed the younger of the two, about twenty.
She had a child's face, luminous, which wore an expression that was dreamy and cheeky at the same time.
When she smiled it seemed she was doing it for posterity:
her eyes were frozen, as if she was posing. When she
didn't smile, her eyes roamed around the room – deci-
phering some secret written on our faces, it felt like –
and every time I looked her straight in the eye, she
answered with a look so profound that I had to look
away, it unnerved me like the dance of two choirs.

'It's for Benares,' Jimi said in a flat, almost off-hand
voice.

Zelda pouted sulkily and then burst into cheerful,
throaty laughter, whilst Mina shook her head and sighed.
But Maman was quick to reassure them: Benares was

the most beautiful village she knew and its inhabitants weren't anywhere near as backward as people made out.

'You see,' she said, pointing at us.

'How much are you asking?' Jimi went on.

'It's seven hundred rupees each,' answered Mina.

'Six hundred,' Jimi protested.

'Seven hundred,' insisted Zelda, and she trained a sombre, penetrating look on Jimi. 'Don't forget that it's for a whole night.'

'Yes, but it's getting on a bit, isn't it?' retorted Jimi, holding his arm out to her and pointing at his watch.

Mayi and Maman didn't seem concerned by the haggling. They were both looking off to one side, out of the window. They were like two lookouts in a hide; they had the same wide, glittering eyes and heads gravely bent forward. Between the parted curtains, I could see moths flattening themselves against the windowpanes or banging into them or flying about the garden from flower to flower. I could see passers-by too and the pools of light that enveloped them whenever a car or a moped passed. On the other side of the street, between a patch of waste ground and a warehouse-type building, there was a crooked old house, at a window of which two silhouetted lovers were holding each other and chewing something as they looked at the sky. If I sank a little deeper into my chair I could see the moon above the house; it looked as if it were edging its way up a mountain.

'How about if we meet halfway?' asked Jimi.

'We can't,' answered Mina, 'this is halfway.'

I thought to myself that seven hundred was fair enough, they don't have an easy job, plus they have to give Maman her cut, it must be fifty-fifty, and I don't like haggling anyway, so I ended up saying, 'That's fair enough, seven hundred rupees.'

We had to hand the money over straightaway, to Maman. Mayi paid, and then sank down in his chair with a long sigh of relief. He was so happy that he smiled at everybody, even at Jimi who looked at him wide-eyed, clearly confused. Maman counted the notes Mayi had given her, and then, swivelling on her chair, turned to me. I put my hand in my trouser pocket and I had such an erection that for a minute I thought I wouldn't be able to get it out again. I told Maman that it'd been like that ever since I'd seen Ma Tante. That made her laugh. She was still laughing when we drove off.

Mayi was still sitting behind me, Mina was next to him and Zelda was further along, behind Jimi. Mina and Zelda were asking questions about Benares, the point of which must have been to draw us out and size us up so that they could reassure themselves: after all they were leaving with three men they'd only just set eyes on and going somewhere they didn't know.

'There's a store,' said Jimi, 'a health clinic, a post office, and a school as well, but only for very little ones.'

'Is that all?' asked Mina.

'And houses of course,' Jimi added with a smile, 'and fields and the sea at the far end.'

'But what about shops? A restaurant?'

'No, you don't get those at Benares,' answered Jimi, as he glanced at a building site that ran alongside the road for several kilometres. There were walls of varying heights and at the base of them, all jumbled up together, cables, hose-pipes, pick-axes, spades, girders and machines that were in the process of being assembled or being taken to pieces. It looked as if a robbery was in progress, even though there were lights all over the place and silhouettes who were silently patrolling. 'For them you have to go to Mahébourg, but Curepipe's even better, because of the choice.'

'So it's not a big place, then,' said Zelda. 'How many of you are there?'

'I don't know exactly,' Jimi replied. 'I guess about two hundred. In the past there used to be a lot more – but then again, in the past there used to be a sugar mill.'

Zelda leaned forward; she seemed to be taking it all very seriously. She raised her hand to her ear as she asked, 'And now?'

'And now,' said Jimi, 'there's only the chimney that's still standing.' He glanced back over his shoulder and gently shook his head. 'It looks like a war memorial since the owners did it up. That was two years ago. They shouldn't have done it – or else they should have done everything up: I mean, the post office, the clinic and the school, of course, because you should see how run down they all are ... They just don't think about the community at all.'

They didn't think about proportions either. They had made that chimney at least ten metres taller when they did it up. Now it was grotesquely outsized, looming over the fields, which it overwhelmed, and the ruins, which it robbed of all their beauty . . .

'So why did they do it up?' asked Zelda. She looked at me with perplexed eyes, murmuring insistently, 'Why?'

I said it must have been so that they'd be remembered as builders. 'All they care about is making sure their names go down in history.'

'They could have shown more restraint,' added Jimi. 'When you think that they shut down the mill and put a whole village out of work . . .'

'How long has it been,' drawled Mina, 'since they shut down the mill?'

'It'll be thirty years in a few months,' answered Jimi. 'The owners thought there were too many mills for so small a cane crop. They said that some had to be shut to reduce their losses. Increase their profits, more like.'

'It's always like that,' muttered Zelda, and she leaned back with a little strangled cry.

The driver of the car following us was in a hurry. He blew his horn full blast; he wanted us to give him some room so he could overtake. Jimi slowed down and hugged the ditch by the roadside. The car overtook easily but then the driver started hooting again; a big lorry blocking his way didn't want to give him any space. So then the two drivers started having it out with each other, leaning on their horns as hard as they could and Jimi joined in, but he was laughing at the same time – he said that it was always like that when there was a wedding. Then we came to a crossroads and each car took a different road. As we went our separate ways the drivers hooted one last time, to say goodbye, I suppose, and I'm sure that deep down it must been affecting for all of them. A look of bitterness flickered across Jimi's face when he stopped hooting and he looked intently all around him as if he were checking something. He ruffled his hair, smoothed it back down and then finally brought his hand to his forehead in an awkward, despairing gesture, 'It was a total disaster when the mill went out of business: the whole village depended on it ... Everybody worked there.'

'You too?' asked Mina.

'Me too,' answered Jimi.

'So what did you do when there was no mill anymore?'

'The same as everyone – everyone who stayed on, that is, because lots of people left Benares to look for work elsewhere ... I jammed my hands in my pockets and paced around the village all day for weeks on end, months even. I'd look at the sky and the mountains, the fields and the mill, of course, the most, but we all looked at the road most. We kept waiting for someone from the Government to arrive who'd help us find work or make the owners see sense. It took us quite a while to realise that no one was going to come. And then Benares felt forsaken, as if it had been abandoned by everyone . . .'

'That can't have been a pretty sight,' said Zelda.

'It wasn't a pretty sight,' continued Jimi without drawing breath. 'It felt as if we'd left the country, as if the sea had suddenly surrounded us and Benares had become an island cut off from the world . . . It really wasn't a pretty sight, I tell you, a whole village adrift. Days just worrying about the weather and counting the hours passing, that'd seem to go on for ever. And then in the evenings, we'd meet up in front of the mill and remember the good old days: dawn, eyes still misty with sleep, starting off on the long walk through the fields; that feeling you always had of being one with the earth and the stones we heaped into piles and the cane we stripped and cut; that heady smell of wormwood which rose up every time it rained and our feet not making any noise as we walked up to the mill in the mud or the powdery dust or through the wild, climbing grass. And the mill was our landmark: we only had to raise our eyes for it to feel closer and us not get lost when the cane was up over our heads. But it was much more than a landmark – it was like a home to us. I remember that every time someone had the chance to get their photo taken, they'd want it to be in front of the mill – that shows you how fond of it we were. But the owners weren't good to us, you should have seen them and heard the way they talked to us. There were only three of them but it sounded like there was a hundred when they shouted their orders that stung like insults and it seems strange when I think about it now, but before I met any tourists I thought all whites were bad . . . But still, we'd always be quick to talk about the past, and when we had exhausted all our memories, we'd look up at the sky and watch the clouds disappearing over the pylons and the rooftops on their way to other peaks and summits, the mountains. Someone once said – I suppose to break the silence, or make us dream a little, think about something different – "Look, they've turned red," but it wasn't true, the mountains hadn't changed colour . . .'

'What colour are they?' asked Zelda. Her voice was strangely husky, almost sad, and her eyes roved back and forth, a distant look in them. She seemed to be searching for the mountains – I suppose to see what colour they were – but it was too dark to see anything. 'I bet they're a beautiful blue . . .'

'They're a beautiful grey,' I answered, 'a dazzling one.' I wanted to add, 'Like your eyes,' because her eyes were sparkling, but they were darker. 'Like a sky that's beginning to clear,' I said, 'after the rain has stopped.'

'What about you,' asked Mina, and she nudged Mayi with her elbow, 'don't you ever talk?'

'Me?' He pretended to think for a moment, then declared emphatically in ringing tones, as if he was in an opera, 'Of course I talk!'

Mina asked him some more questions. Mayi said that he liked games, especially cards and football, and that he could play them for hours on end and that he did so a lot. But football was his favourite; cards sometimes gave him a headache.

'I've played football too,' said Mina, 'but I haven't played for ages.'

'What position did you play?' asked Mayi.

'I always used to be in goal,' answered Mina. 'That's why I haven't played for ages. I used to get shouted at every time I let in a goal, when I was only doing it to help them out in the first place because no one else wanted to be goalkeeper.'

'I'm the same,' said Mayi, 'I don't like being shouted at when I'm playing, it puts me in a daze and then I make even more mistakes.'

Mina gave a faint smile and looked curiously at Mayi's face. 'I've got a son who plays football as well,' she said in a low voice as if she was afraid of being heard, 'he's very like you.'

'What position does he play?' asked Mayi.

'He plays on the wings,' answered Mina, 'sometimes on the left, sometimes on the right, and oh, he can run so fast when he's got the ball, it's amazing the way he spins and twists past the people trying to stop him getting to goal, I swear, he's just like a little angel . . .' Her voice had got louder and louder, she was almost shouting at one point, and now her whole body was trembling. Her shoulders especially, little nervous twitches that made her seem sickly. Probably as a way to stop herself moving about any more, she put her elbows on her knees and cupped her face in her hands, and then she looked at Mayi for a long time, as if she was expecting a sign of approval from him, some reassurance. But not a word, not a gesture from him – he seemed lost in his thoughts, a distant, almost uninterested, look in his eyes. Finally she asked in a weak, monotonous voice, as if all the silence had exhausted her, 'So what position do you play?'

'Normally midfield,' Mayi answered, 'but most of the time I end up at the back defending, because everyone else has gone up front to try and score, apart from the keeper of course . . .'

'But when the others go off,' asked Mina, 'don't they come back again?'

'Either they don't come back at all, or if they do, they're so tired they're not much use and sometimes they actually get in the way.'

'If I was you,' said Mina, 'I'd be like them, I'd go and try and score as well.'

'Yes, but it wouldn't be much of a game then . . . And there's the keeper to think of too, I couldn't leave him on his own, he's a friend of mine.'

'Well then you should change team,' said Mina, 'otherwise you'll never be able to play in your proper position.'

Mayi swayed his head gently from side to side. 'That's what I think as well, but my grandfather doesn't want me to play outside Benares, he's afraid I'll get hurt and that I won't be able to work.'

'Because no one ever gets hurt in Benares?' asked Mina.

'Not really,' Mayi replied. 'A few sprains, that's all. Whereas if you get a proper football injury, it can sometimes take months before you really recover.'

Then she asked him what he did. He said that he was a fisherman, but that he hadn't been doing it for long.

'Now I'm hungry, all of a sudden,' said Mina.

'That's lucky,' said Mayi, 'I've got some fish at home, I fried it up earlier this evening.'

'How about you,' Zelda asked me, 'what do you do?' She had begun to seem more and more like a child: her face of course, but her voice and her gestures as well – for instance the way she grabbed my arm and craned her neck forward when she talked to me. 'How old are you?' I asked her. 'You're not twenty, are you?' She immediately let go of my arm and screwed up her face, "Course not,' she said and then shrugged her shoulders triumphantly, 'Sixteen, that's all.' The expression on her face hovered somewhere between rapture and euphoria, without blossoming into either. But her mouth was wide open, framing milk-white teeth that lined up like beams of light. 'How about you, don't you want to tell me what you do?' she insisted gently, leaning forward, then back, and finally pressing up against the back of Jimi's seat. She smelled of sour apple and leaf mould, it was a mixture of sweat and perfume with a musky smell of wilted flowers, ones that had fallen to the bottom of the vase and been forgotten. I said that I was a garage-hand in a garage in Mahébourg. She didn't think I was telling the truth, maybe because I'd been slow to answer, and she asked to see my hands. 'They're clean,' she said, touching them, and then sniffing them. 'Those aren't mechanic's hands.' I explained that we wore gloves now; it'd been like that for a few years. She still didn't want to believe me but she laughed wholeheartedly, like Mina.

My neck was beginning to ache from turning round. I decided to keep looking ahead as I talked, like Jimi, for a while. Outside, there was a strange sense of empti-ness and endlessness about the sky and the countryside alike. As far as the eye could see we might as well have been in a desert. It was like a painting: even though it was flashing past our windows, the entire landscape was absolutely still. Not a star moving in the sky, not a breeze stirring the bushes by the roadside or the fields in the distance. Nothing but the heavy, torpid air and the inertia that lay in wait for us all. I'd have liked not to be in the car, just for long enough to watch it driving through that sleepy countryside and, bringing it to life. It's different when you're inside; motion is less tangible.

I asked Jimi to stop at Curepipe; I only had a couple of cigarettes left. He nodded and yawned as he did so, and he smiled when he saw I was watching him. It was crumpled, that smile, from another generation, and unreal that face that rose and fell as its wrinkles pleased. They were deep but soft looking, his wrinkles, like waves. He yawned again as he parked the car. He couldn't have had that much sleep recently; his eyes were red and puffy with tiredness.

'Anyone want anything?'

Mina wanted some mints, she was starting to feel queasy – it was the same every time she got in a car –

and Zelda wanted a packet of cigarettes, she didn't mind what sort.

The street looked like a waiting room. Men, most of them young, were strolling about in the way people do when they're going round in circles, the sort of motion that doesn't really get you anywhere, that's almost a prison in itself. They seemed indifferent to everything except their footsteps, which they stared at fixedly. Perhaps they were on the game and were waiting for clients who were late – I thought of the sailors caught up in some fight that was going on and on – or maybe they just didn't have enough money to go anywhere else, such as a restaurant. They weren't very talkative, either way, and some even looked depressed; you're bound to feel like that sooner or later if you go round in circles. 'On, on,' I said to myself, and pushed, then pulled the door of the restaurant, saying 'It's fine' to the doorman who had stood up, and then sat down again. It was a child. The look he gave me seemed to brim over, probably because his pupils were so big they almost filled his eyes. He showed me his plate as if asking to be excused: suppertime.

I ran up the steps; the restaurant was on the first floor. There were only three customers, each at a separate table. The owner was on his own as well, sitting on a bar stool behind the bar. His clothes were a mess:

he was wearing a shirt with holes in it and brown stains around the collar and his trousers were all crumpled and the flies gaped where they were missing a button.

'Evening,' I said to him. 'Can I have two packets of Bristol?'

'Tens or twenties?'

'Tens.'

He took two packets out of a drawer, wiped them with a cloth, but then put them on the bar, which was dirty and wet. The floor was wet too; there were even puddles of water in places and cockroaches zigzagging from one puddle to the next. In a corner, near a door that looked blocked up, there was a pile of buckets, bricks and planks and an old bicycle that had lost its wheels and was draped with clothes that had holes and brown stains on them.

'And ten mints.'

While the owner was totting up what I owed him, a customer told him he was going out but that he wouldn't be long and he went out of the restaurant scuffing his feet. When I saw him again, he was strolling unhurriedly down the steps, smoking a cigarette. I looked at him as I went past, but he wasn't the person I'd been thinking of, someone I'd met at a dance the week before. He just looked like him from a distance and from the back. The doorman opened the door, he didn't have his plate anymore, and as he said goodbye to me, his face seemed naked: his eyes were shut. 'I hope you have a good night too,' I answered.

I lit a cigarette and kept my eyes fixed on it; we were driving through a village I found it hard to look at – all along its streets all there were were shops, one after the other, without any break between them. Every shop had its posters and its billboards and every sign had its brightly coloured, flashy images. Jimi thought it was funny the way, after all that, everything still managed to look so dreary and bleak. He said it was to do with appearances that whole artificial, deceptive side. I chucked out the cigarette at the edge of the village just as some cars overtook us. They must have been rushing off to the airport; they took the Mahébourg road, and we took the Britannia one. It's one of the most deserted roads I know. I've only seen someone on it once – a man who had got lost, and who Jimi took home to Savannah. I leaned my elbows on the window and peered at the fields as they sped past. You could see thin silhouettes that were bent flat by the wind or whisked away like flickering shadows, some smoke sometimes and piles of black stones on the horizon, but mainly you could hear things, all sorts of different sounds. There were some that it felt I was hearing for the first time, and they seemed as mysterious as an obscure idiom. I thought of moles and bats and all the other things that live in the dark. I even thought about vampires and what sort of cries they might make. Then I'd had enough of scanning the night, so I turned towards Jimi. He was calmly working the steering wheel and staring gravely at the road: there were no other cars but it was full of bends. Just as I was about to tell him that he could pull over and have a rest because he was yawning and sighing the whole time, I shut my mouth and turned round instead. Mayi was looking out of the window into the darkness. Beads of sweat stood out on his gaunt cheeks and something like content-ment, amusement shone in his eyes. Zelda, her head tilted to one side, was smiling and listening to Mina who was talking to her softly. I didn't know what she was talking about; her voice was just a faint, mean-ingless hum. Then she fell silent and when she cuddled up to Mayi, Zelda lit a cigarette and looked out at the fields where a blurry flock was grazing. I waited for her to turn back before asking, 'How would it make you feel to live somewhere and know there was somewhere else with the same name in a different country?'

Zelda took the cigarette out of her mouth and shook her head. 'Maybe it would make me travel.' She smiled sheepishly. 'Why?'

'Because there's a place called Benares in India as well,' I said.

She stared at me for a long time with a look in her eye that was somehow vague and absorbed at the same time, as if she was asking herself lots of questions, and then she leaned towards me, mouth first, and murmured, fascinated, 'Have you been there?'

'Last year,' I said, 'in August.'

'So what's Benares like? Is it a village too?'

I said that it's a town and that it's sacred to Hindus and I asked her if she knew why. Her eyes began ferreting about, glittering suddenly, but she didn't know. 'Because Hindus believe they'll go to paradise if they die in Benares . . .' I expected her to look at me wide-eyed in amazement or get the giggles but she just smiled and shyly swayed her head. 'And that's how it's been for centuries,' I went on, 'lots of people head there as soon as they feel the first signs of death. They leave their homes and their families and embark on what are sometimes very long, arduous journeys just so they can die in Benares and be sure of going to paradise . . .'

'Even if they're criminals?' asked Zelda. 'Do they go to paradise too?'

I said sure, even if they're criminals, because the only thing that matters is dying in Benares.

'Well that's cruel, then,' mumbled Zelda and she stayed silent for a minute, before asking, 'What about all the people who die somewhere else who aren't criminals?'

'It's only cruel if you believe in paradise. If you don't . . .'

'Even so, it's not fair.'

I tried to make her understand that dying's not about paradise, it's not about anything at all, but she didn't want to know. She rolled down the window and looked at the sky that was clearing above us. Only a few clouds were left and they were no threat to anyone, they were too far apart. What about Benares? I elbowed Jimi as I leaned forward to look and then did so again, more sharply, as I leaned back up. Not a single star, nothing but blackness shrouding everything, even the line of the horizon. It was unnerving how much the sky had been able to change in such a short time. But what threw me most was Zelda's silence and I wracked my brains for something to say so that she'd start talking to me again.

The car crawled forward, struggling up a half-cultivated hill. When we reached the top, I leaned towards her and said in my most distinguished voice,

'They're strange things, stars, aren't they, but the fact is they're made of just the same stuff as us ... When we look at a star it's as if we're looking at ourselves.'

Zelda looked round and asked if I could repeat what I'd just said, she hadn't heard the beginning. She moved closer and listened to me with an engrossed expression. When I finished, a glint of amusement shone in her eyes, which she quickly dispelled with a few flutters of her eyelids. 'You mean they've got a brain like us, a heart?'

'Could be,' I said, half-laughing. 'Why not a penis as well?'

She started laughing, like me, a happy, ringing laugh, then she cleared her throat and, opening her eyes wide, asked, 'Is Benares as strange as a star?'

I looked at my watch and then the road, both furtive, reflex glances, and then I said that everything in Benares had seemed strange to me. 'First just the fact that people believe a story like that – you should see all those people who are dying arriving from everywhere the whole time, by train, boat, rickshaw, car and plane when they come from far away, from another country. There are even buses just for the dying, that come from neighbouring towns and have very graphic names, *The Paradise Express*, *The Last Journey*, *The End*.' Then I talked about the dying themselves and I said how old

and ill and poor most of them are. 'You see them everywhere just waiting to die,' and I thought for a second
about what one would do in a situation like that, 'and
while they wander through the dark, twisting little streets
of the old city or else they sit under giant sunshades
and spend the time they've got left gazing at the Ganges.
They look as if they're lazing around, they could be at
the beach . . . But mainly you see them at the temples
and other holy places where they queue up for a prayer
or a blessing. They seem as if they're not there at all,
indifferent to the slow-moving lines that sometimes are
more than a kilometre long. Nothing around them exists
anymore, neither the rain, nor the air that's black with
smoke, nor the boiling sun. They're all you see, alone
with their gods, alone on this earth that will no longer
nurture them like a mother. They're a little like the
houses in Benares, exhausted by all they've been through,
worn out by the heat and the monsoons, cracked . . .
Not to mention the poverty they have to suffer and the
injustices they have to endure at the hands of their
fellow men – you should see how they're treated sometimes, like dogs squabbling over scraps who people kick
or beat with sticks. Maybe that's why they long for paradise so intently and trust in their gods so much, as if
the gods were the humiliated's only hope, their self-
respect. And in fact it's thinking of their gods that gives

them the strength to carry on living and keep going from one temple to the next and not let themselves drown when they bathe in the Ganges. They'd be so quick to choose such an easy death if their religion allowed them.'

'The poor things,' Zelda said softly, 'and just before they die, too,' and even more quietly, almost in a murmur, 'That's what's so sad, to have to live off scraps at that age and be treated like dogs, along with everything else they have to go through, because I'm sure there's more . . .'

We were like two friends meeting up after a long separation, two travellers swapping stories from their wanderings, a few memories to enliven the late-night road. I thought to myself that stories must be what we travel for, to have something to tell the people we love. While I rummaged through my pockets and took out my lighter and cigarettes, I looked vaguely at the sea and the meadow running down to it, full of stones and sleeping oxen. Pale glimmers, like beacons, flickered in the distance. I thought of fishermen out smuggling, signalling to each other. Who else could it be at this time? I lit a cigarette and passed it to Zelda. She took a deep drag and gave it back, shaking her head. 'My mouth tastes bitter.'

Outside everything was grey: the road, the fields, the houses, even the people. Which doesn't mean that in fact there were tiny patches of red or blue or yellow – the patches were grey as well. But still it wasn't a uniform grey; in some places it was brighter, in others it had a golden tinge or was almost black or greenish. And everything was harmonious. Even the sounds, and yet they weren't alike at all. Sounds of men talking, scuffling or falling flat on their backs; sounds of bicycles and breaking glass; the roar of lorries; the sound of dogs especially, who were fighting as much as the men, just as aggressively, and moaning just as plaintively when the fights were over; the engine's revs as Jimi turned off the main road to take a short-cut; the wind buffeting the doors and the tyres squealing at the gentlest bend. Everything made you feel sleepy and as if you were going round in circles. Maybe because there was something never-ending about the roads, like a labyrinth, and maybe because I was tired anyway and in a hurry to get back. I thought about the house, the yard plunged in darkness and the dogs that would be mooching around it. What if it rained? Well, they just had to take shelter under the tree and pace around that while they waited for it to stop. I paced around with them for a minute, then I decided to have a little sleep and forget how tired I was but I had barely closed my eyes when someone shook my arm. Not Jimi, he was busy watching the road. I craned my head to one side and looked over my shoulder. It was Zelda. She wanted to know if I'd told the people in Benares that there was somewhere in our country with the same name. I looked at her for a long time without thinking of anything, as if I was hanging over a sheer drop. Gradually I started thinking about the tree again and the house and the dogs and I nodded my head several times, 'Yes, but I only told some people, the ones I really liked, who I could talk to.' Zelda smiled at first, then she frowned suddenly and stared at me with great accusing eyes. They seemed to be reproaching me for not having given a full enough answer. But what more could I say? I turned my face away from hers and looked at the road in the weak light of the headlights. In my mind's eye I saw the Ganges and the sandalwood and wilted flowers slowly floating down the river, and then some of the faces of the people who kneel all day in prayer, and the faces of the dying who sleep on the streets when they've been thrown out of old people's homes because they're the wrong caste, and the clothes they wear when they're dead, the same as those of the children who sell garlands and who hassle pilgrims and tourists for a few rupees. Everything came back to me in the usual order. 'Sometimes,' I said, turning round, 'I wonder if I didn't go to Benares just for their sakes, so that one day they can do the same journey themselves.'

'What did they think of that?' Zelda asked.

'They liked it a lot,' I said. 'For one of them, it was like a blinding revelation when he found out, as if he'd personally discovered an unknown land. Every time we saw each other he'd tell me he'd never have thought it, that there could be another Benares, and it unnerved him, there being two places with the same name that are so far apart, so different, and he felt proud to live in one of them, maybe because it gave him the feeling of opening up to the world, of becoming part of some sort of network which must have seemed pretty vast and mysterious, which he'd never suspected existed until then . . .'

'I can understand him being blown away,' said Zelda. 'I'd have been the same, just thinking about it, I mean, where do you start?'

'There was someone else who told me he'd been seeing double ever since. I suppose he meant feeling drunk or something like that. Whatever it was, this whole thing seemed even stranger to him than paradise . . . And of course they all asked me over and over again to tell them about the other Benares, the one they didn't know.'

'What did you tell them about?' asked Zelda.

'A bit about everything,' I answered. 'First about what you can see before you get to the village, when you see it in the distance. I told them about the mill and the road that leads to it. About the huge fields and the roofs of some of the houses that rise above the cane. And about the sea off in the distance and the huge skies. Then I told them about the village itself. About the school, the store and the houses that are so far from the sea. And about the people of course, how they live and what jobs they have and how much time they spend doing nothing because there isn't much that happens in Benares . . . Sometimes I was bombarded with so many questions that I didn't know what answers to give any more, it felt as if I'd said everything, so then I'd lie, I'd make up landscapes, I'd try to get their imaginations working too. I'd tell them about the sky when there's a storm, how it builds up and up until lightning bursts it like an abscess, or about the sea in summer, how we look at it when there hasn't been any rain for months, just sunshine all day long, and I'd tell them how it looks like a huge mirror, how it shines and reflects up at the sky . . .'

'You could go on all night, you two,' Mina inter-rupted, adding in a falsetto voice, 'What I'd like is for someone to explain to me how come there are two Benareses.' She stared at me and scratched her head, as if she was remembering a painful event that still upset her. She had a virginal expression, I mean an expres-sion I didn't recognise on her, it was sad and fierce at the same time, like a wildcat that's been hurt, offended.

I shrugged my head and my shoulders in the same movement, the way you do when you're hesitating between different answers, but my voice was completely assured. 'It happened a long time ago, over two hundred years.'

'Yes, but how?' asked Mina impatiently.

I looked away slightly and lied, 'It's too long ago for anybody to remember properly,' then I slumped down in my seat, I felt exhausted, drained and sad all of a sudden, like you do at the end of something.

The rain had stopped but you could still feel it in the air and the sky hung so low that it seemed to flatten everything, even the mountains. The fields kept on flashing past with their scarecrows, their gleaming canals and their paths that disappeared into the darkness. We drove alongside a river, a copse and a water tower that stood in the middle of a field of maize and then we entered Savannah. Built on the side of a hill, the village was criss-crossed with sunken, bumpy lanes, lined on both sides by houses that listed towards the valley. At the corner of one of the lighter lanes in the village, two men were leaning against a shop front. They were looking at another pair who were squatting under a tree and playing cards in the faint light of a streetlight. They seemed to be waiting for the game to end, probably to start a new one together. All four had haggard faces, which seemed familiar but I didn't have enough time to be sure. A dog with a shaggy coat shot out of the next lane. He looked like an old lion, with a mane of white hair standing up on the back of his neck. He chased us to the edge of the village, and then left us for another car, which was coming from the opposite direction and hooting. He started running and barking again, but more intensely than before; it must have been because the people in the other car had challenged him by yapping, in their own way, and baying at the moon.

'Can't we listen to something else?' asked Zelda.

Jimi turned on the radio, but not for long, there was only men talking among themselves about things that were hard for us to follow.

'We should have listened from the start,' said Jimi when he turned off the radio. 'Anyway I need to stop

and fill up,' and he stopped a few metres on at a petrol
station. Mina and Zelda got out. They wanted to have
a little walk, stretch their legs. They straightened their
clothes and looked at their feet as they walked round
the petrol station. They walked along by a patch of
waste ground and some houses, then they crossed the
street by a pale, solitary streetlight and suddenly disappeared round a bend.

'Why did you tell them that you'd been to Benares
in India?' Mayi asked me.

'I don't know,' I answered. 'It just came out . . .
Was that wrong?'

Mayi shrugged his shoulders and grimaced, but
didn't say anything.

I rolled down the window and looked at the petrol
station. It was an old building shaped like an upturned
bucket, with curving walls that narrowed towards the
top. Two men were standing near the door, leaning
against an old, open-top jeep. One was wearing a light
suit and talking a lot. The other was fat and wore shiny
shoes, grey tight-fitting trousers and an orange and white
striped shirt that was open to his chest. He had his
hands behind his back and was nodding constantly as
he listened – there weren't going to be any complaints
from him, that was for sure. On the white wall, just
above the picture window, you could see finger marks,

streaks of mud and soot. In one of the rooms of the petrol station, an old, dark complexioned man with round cheeks was sitting at a vast metal table. He was writing or doing calculations, bent over a thick note-book and some loose sheets of paper. With a wave of his pen, he signalled to us to wait, while with his other hand he meticulously arranged the bits of paper and the notebook.

'Do you have a favourite?' Mayi asked, pointing to Mina and Zelda who were slowly coming back up the street.

'No,' I answered. 'How about you?'

A glint flashed in his eyes, 'I like Mina a lot.'

'That's good,' I said with delight. 'I feel the same about Zelda.'

Jimi was telling Mina and Zelda the name of every village we drove through, but all you saw of them were doors and lit-up windows and grey shadows hugging the walls and house fronts. The houses seemed empty, abandoned years ago. But those outlines on the walls, those screens over the doors? Ghosts, I thought to myself, the night is filled with ghosts. It was an absurd thought, but no more so than Jimi's litany of names. When we were driving between the villages, he'd lean out of the window and watch the mountains gliding gently by from left to right. Maybe he was looking for the meaning of the name he had just said, or maybe he was simply taking a break before getting back to his geography.

'How about you two?' I asked Mina and Zelda, 'are you both from Sainte Croix itself?'

'I am, yes,' answered Mina and she looked at Zelda who was already nodding in agreement, 'She's from Pamplemousses.'

'That's a place I know well,' I said. 'I've got a friend who lives there, just by the church.'

'What's he called?' asked Zelda. 'Maybe I know him.'

'Samuel,' I said. 'Do you know him?'

Zelda repeated the name, enunciating each syllable, and then she shook her head in an embarrassed way. 'What's he like? Has he got long or short hair?'

'He's missing a few teeth,' I said, 'the top ones mainly, and he has quite long hair with a parting that's often crooked. And when he walks, he bends over double like a hunchback and his whole body leans forward towards the ground, I don't know why and you always think he's going to fall over at any minute but he never does . . . do you know who I mean?'

Zelda moved closer to me, 'Samuel what?'

'I don't know,' I answered. 'I've never asked.'

'Do you know where he works, at least?'

'He's a bricklayer,' I said, 'but it depends, sometimes he sells vegetables at the market, or fruit.'

Zelda shook her head, 'No, I really can't think . . . It's been so long since I've been home,' and she started counting on her fingers, 'It's been more than six months . . . But I'll ask the next time I go.'

'It's a place I like very much,' I said, 'especially at night, when there's no one out any more. Then it's like being in a real desert.'

Zelda brushed back her hair that was falling into her eyes and turned towards me, twisting her handbag in her hands and trying to look friendly, 'I don't like deserts: they're too hot and you never see anybody.'

The landscape now was just a plain, stretching un-relievedly on and on, as if we were driving along the line of the horizon. I lit two cigarettes, one for Jimi, and looked at the road and thought about tomorrow; I was wondering whether I'd go to work or not. I could say I was ill, that I'd got a bad dose of the 'flu. 'My boss wouldn't believe me, though, no way,' I thought, 'and he'll be pissed off with me, he could even threaten me with the sack. Oh well, he can just sack me then, can't he? I'll find another garage or else I'll change job. But not as a fisherman or a gardener. I'm too scared of drowning and I know my brain would explode if I had to work in the sun for too long.' I was quietly mulling over some ques-tions about being a plumber, such as how much I could earn a month and which villages would be good to start looking for clients in, when suddenly there were a succes-sion of cries outside that sounded like squeals, short and piercing. A wounded animal probably, crying or calling for help. I thought of a dog that had been run over, and I thought how that must feel, to be crushed, then aban-doned. A few kilometres on we heard it whimpering again. It was weird, it couldn't be following us.

'What is that?' I asked Jimi.

He rolled down the window and scanned the road and the countryside like someone searching for clues. Which he found, I suppose, because he turned to me with a smile that lit up his face. 'It's beaters letting the hunters know there's an animal around. But I don't know what sort. A stag, maybe, or a boar.'

'But don't they scare off the animals, high-pitched calls like that?'

'No, I think they paralyse them, actually,' Jimi answered and started yawning, then coughing and he stopped smiling after he felt his forehead. 'I wonder if I've got a temperature.'

'You should have a mint,' Mina suggested and insisted he have one immediately.

Jimi crunched the sweet and said he felt much better. 'It's true,' he added and, as if to reassure her, he whistled a tune that seemed to spread out across the plain, it was so jolly and deep. Then, after hugging a long bend, he suddenly took a left-hand turn and called out, 'Benares!' It sounded like the end of a game, or when rehearsals have finished.

'The fields are huge,' said Zelda. 'They're all you see, along with the sky and the road of course.'

The road looked like a Roman road. It was straight and broad. And lined with sugar cane in flower.

'There, that's the mill chimney,' Jimi said, slowing down. 'What do you think?'

'It really is just like a war memorial,' answered Mina, a slight quaver in her voice. 'It sends shivers up my spine.'

Of the mill itself only the floor was left. It was cracked in places but spotless, as if it had just been washed, cleaned. 'This is where we play football,' I said, 'and before we start a game we sweep up all the straw that blows in from the fields,' and I pointed out the goalposts. Behind one of them you could see all of Benares.

IN BABYLON

When I was a child and I'd come home late, my father used to say, 'What have you been doing in Babylon this time?' I wouldn't answer, I'd just hang my head and go to my room – I used to feel so ashamed when I got told off. Because 'to be in Babylon' is a pejorative expression. It means roam, wander and so stray from one's path.

Hassan is thinking of the quickest way; he wants to show me a part of town that has been bombed. He folds up his newspaper and puts it in his pocket as we cross a street shaded by shop awnings. His face stiffens; he scans the sky for a moment and warns me that it won't be pretty. I try to reassure him, saying there are wars in my country too. He blurts out something but I don't insist. I look around me, fascinated, wondering where that music can be coming from – maybe from that boat going down the river. It looks like a floating discotheque.

These people and this place seem familiar to me: gourds on mats, rubble strewn between buildings; children sitting in circles hawking big gobs of spit onto the ground or over bay hedges; whiffs of urine and sheep fat rising up from tightly packed shacks that are black with grime. I see dead rats lying in a patch of sun, a queue zigzagging up to a bus stop and a cloud of flies gathering on a dog's eye. We walk faster under some scaffolding and hear hoarse, raised voices, arguing and spinning stories in little restaurants with only one table and a vase of paper flowers; the ashtrays are tin-plate and most of the lamps are broken.

A man shuts the door of one of these establishments and looks up and down the street with an amused expression. Then he thrashes the air with his arms, as if he's parrying punches; he's wearing a vest and Terylene trousers. He brings his bike out of the bushes and pushes it round the square, taking small, shuffling steps. 'He's trying to sober up,' I say, 'and get himself together before he goes home.' Or maybe he's just clowning around and having fun. Hassan carries on telling me the names of the streets and the buildings and going through the history, the dictatorship and the embargo, but nothing he says is as vivid as the people we meet and the way they express themselves or their livelihoods if they have work. He talks so fast that sometimes I feel he's making fun of me.

He says the thing that infuriates him the most is seeing all these kids left to their own devices; that never used to happen before the war. They play with bits of string, clippings of metal and leather; they dig in the dirt with sharp stones and plant banana skins and orange peel in the driveways of building sites. They suddenly disappear behind a bush and the next thing you know you can hear them wiping themselves with a handful of grass.

'They're like orphans,' Hassan adds in a low voice, 'with no one to them to confide in.'

A dog scampers off down a muddy street. A cattle truck turns and skids like a sledge and a simpleton counts passers-by in a loud voice. You can see his gums and his wobbly gold teeth. He is perched on a crate, beaming blissfully in all directions. Hassan lights a cigarette and dives into a dark tunnel.

'Dogs,' he says hurriedly, 'they're the first to get it too.'

In the half-light, it seems as if we've emerged in a village. People are carrying grass on their shoulders, buckets of water and rusty iron rods, which they drag along the ground. Others are splitting rocks with pick-axes or smoking with a bored air, leaning their backs against a wooden shebeen. In the background ducks are paddling about in a murky canal and hens are pecking at piles of rubbish amid a flurry of dust.

Hassan flicks the barbed wire fence with a stick: of course he'd like to leave the country one day and see what it's like in other places with all those strange customs. He seems lost in his dreams of the bush, so absorbed that he looks drowsy, exhausted.

I ask him what's in the paper. He's unfolded it at a bend in the road to fan himself and then rolled it up lengthwise and used it to point out the station buildings.

Today's news is that the leader is in good health, Zorba is a hundred and Sara has got her diploma; there's also a lecture about the youth not abandoning the traditional ways. Sara is in a scout uniform, surrounded by provisions and paraffin lamps. She has a mischievous little face, even if one can't see her eyes because of the dark blotches on the photo.

Branches, plastic bottles and bits of grey cardboard float past under the bridge. Someone groans as they walk away from the river with their tub and a girl spreads out the clothes she has just washed on the grass. She has creamy white arms and hair tied up in a blue scarf. Frilly little garments have been hung on a bush and a sheet is changing shape on the branches of a guava tree.

Men in mud-spattered boots collect kindling on the riverbank, children run after a taxi and street traders selling coloured drinks shout over one another at the tops of their voices, their glasses set out in a circle on silver and black-striped cloths. Some women wait in silence by the entrance to the old Customs building; one of them gets to her feet and brushes her trousers to get rid of some dust or stop them getting creased. She has teddy-bear brown eyes and teeth flecked with lipstick. They seem peaceful, these women, prepared for a long wait before they're let in.

His face inscrutable, a little boy whacks a bush with

a drumstick. 'Will you stop it? Just stop it!' He has a sleepy voice, tired eyes and is wearing pyjamas with white and purple flowers on them. He looks over his shoulder at the barred windows and the drawn silver paper curtains behind him: he is alone with his bush and his other toys scattered around the courtyard. He gives a despairing moan and clasps his head in his hands, 'Why did you do that? Why did you?'

Hassan strides through the bags and old rags cluttering the pavements with such a swinging step that it feels as if he could walk across Baghdad without a break, despite the stifling heat and stink of sewerage and constant noise. But there's beauty even on roads that lead nowhere. He shows me a bricklayer on his ladder which is as spectacular as a pyramid, and that man pushing his barrow from stall to stall, we should stop him and ask him what he's selling or buying – but then suddenly a lorry hurtles past at top speed and we drift off into a daydream watching the two boys in the back, who are clinging to iron bars, their legs splayed.

In the distance an expanse of green wood appears alongside a stretch of river and a hillside dotted with stands of trees that shield huge mansions and their outbuildings from the road. 'That's another country starting,' Hassan says, 'where only the price of the dollar matters.' The kings of ketchup and the underworld live

there with their staff and courtesans. Closer to, the fields
are criss-crossed with low walls and the streets cramped,
overcrowded. The people navigating them remind me
of acrobats or dancers.

That man at the bottom of the flight of steps must
be the groom; he holds a *keffiyeh* in one white-gloved
hand and a bunch of violets in the other. He smiles and
leans to the side and his eyes become two white circles
as he kisses the bride. The guests break into wild applause
and raise their glasses with a triumphant air. In the
stone-paved courtyard, what must be the patriarch of
the family stumbles sleepily and has to hang onto a
wooden post in order not to fall. He tries to turn over
some cardboard boxes with his stick and ends up sliding
them under the extending table with his foot. The gate
slowly closes behind the newlyweds; splashes of colour
pass by on the pavements and I see people waving their
handkerchiefs on a balcony.

Hassan takes a few steps backwards and casts an
expressionless glance down the intersecting street. He's
heard a muffled clatter of scrap metal, which he thinks
might be a lorry rolling. I strain my ears to hear over a
stack of wood being lifted by sling, but the only sound
I can make out is a car backfiring and I carry on walking
towards a dilapidated footbridge full of holes.

'They happen every day though,' Hassan says as he

catches me up by the closed ticket offices of a cinema, 'and then there are fights in the street because people get killed or injured.'

From here we can see men in a square drinking beer from the bottle, cows with their tails in the air, nudging aside bits of paper as they graze on the grass, and a succession of alleys that fall sheer to a parched plain. We hear the rustle of clothes under a carriage entrance and passionate sighs from behind a wall dividing the cul-de-sac from an orchard full of flowers. Another couple march off in the direction of the arcades, cursing the dogs and children running about everywhere. Hassan sniffs some cheap cafés that reek of the sea, and past transports of delight flash across his mind.

We pass a sentry box stippled with grey, a tramp swathed in wrapping paper and some dogs that are rooted to the spot – terrified by our voices and enormous shadows, I suppose. Hassan tells me about his parents as he watches a woman walking towards a railway bridge. 'My mother has given up translating,' he says. 'Because it's been made illegal for a start, and then also because she's had to sell practically all her books.'

Through the fence we can see an open window and a man leaning his elbows on the sill, keeping an eye on his children. They are looking for something in the grass, near a jasmine bush, or else they're burying a dead animal. When they straighten up, they catch sight of us and give us little waves goodbye, as they slowly walk along the other side of the fence.

It looks like a raid: doors are being stacked in a police van. 'Or an extortion racket,' murmurs Hassan who has few illusions. Standing off to one side on his own, a clean-shaven policeman is watching a girl in jeans and flannel shirt walk past a patch of brownish grass and a row of corrugated-iron shacks in the background that look like a painting. She goes over to a lad in a battered cap who is gliding in lazy circles on roller-skates. I look around to get my bearings: a tannery, some pine trees, people grinding flax and the hotel which seems as far away as the other edge of a world robbed of perspective.

Someone calls from the porch, and then steps, of a house to a child who is hanging around by the clothes market. Ali just shrugs and carries on staring at three face cards painted on a white wall, all of them spades, that screw up their eyes through the smoke – King, Queen and the Devil himself.

We stop at the corner of the street and look at a picture of Saddam hanging from a street-lamp. 'He's everywhere,' Hassan says, 'rewriting history.' Saddam is wearing a check shirt and trousers held up by a piece of string. Rake in hand, he's smiling amongst a profusion of flowers and apples the size of melons. I start to think of someone in our village who we call Saddam, because of his moustache and his big mouth, when a clatter of rattling windowpanes makes me duck my head. An old crone gets off a bus, holding a handkerchief over her mouth. As she walks past a rag-and-bone man's stall, she spits a fruit stone out of the side of her mouth, and it rolls into the ditch.

I glance around repeatedly, as if I'm keeping watch on people's movements and their postures, and at the same time I listen to Hassan and ask him whatever questions come into my head, without really thinking. Sometimes we don't understand each other immediately; we stumble over words, which we repeat and dissect until suddenly we burst out laughing when we realise that we've been talking nonsense.

'As for my father,' he says, rubbing his eyes, 'the war has really shaken him. He chain-smokes and spends all day on the balcony staring into space, even though he always used to be the one who'd put everybody in a good mood at home.'

Lying on a bench in a park, a man is talking in his sleep. It's hard to follow his train of thought; he speaks too fast. He has a booming voice and tattooed fingers pressing his eyes shut. His bench is a safe distance from the water splashing in a fountain where a couple of bored children are twisting one another's wrists and another two are grabbing each other by the hair. A mother is leaning on a windowsill, her bracelets clashing threateningly as she gesticulates at the children, whilst the fathers slip away down a goat path and disappear into the scrub.

We walk downhill on the shady side of the street. Hassan lets himself go and catches his breath behind me with a noise like moaning wind. I slow down under a porch and listen to the murmur of a drunken man's singing.

'It's the heat,' he says, 'starting to kill all its people.'

We can see the river again and the boats plying back and forth between its banks. Behind a barge piled high with bales, a pirogue with sails aloft lets itself drift on the current, bobbing up and down like a cork on the dirty, grey water.

A soldier is standing sentry on the roof of a building. He is gazing musingly at the city walls and his resolute bearing and that scarf wrapped round his head have a dignity that reminds me of the Bedouin. Hassan takes my arm and leads me along the river wall. We see smoke on the opposite bank, minarets rising above the trees and a rocky path which dogs are scampering up and down. It makes you feel you have travelled back in time, the sound of the noria and all these rafts, these water buffaloes. And that man walking with a stoop, he could be a Bavarian in national dress: shorts, braces and hat.

Men are slamming their car doors in a fury and shouting in the midst of some stationary cars. They sport a variety of moustaches – washed-out, toothbrush, pimp-style – and the air rings to shouts of son of a bitch, scum, faggot, guinea pig. They shake their clenched fists one last time and then set off again under the golden peaks, a haggard look on their faces.

The girl's expression when our eyes meet, slightly glassy-eyed, a grimy finger at her open mouth – she must be wondering what I'm doing around here. A silhouette is drowsing in a corner, wrapped in a torn bit of cloth, almost touching the vaulted ceiling supported by a row of pillars. The daughter is wearing a dress with a gold collar, blue plastic sandals and she is shining a pocket torch under a table covered in earthenware bowls and cups.

From a distance Hassan acknowledges an uncle who is the worse for *arak* and looks like he's about to have to face the music. The man has strong features, enormous eyes that radiate kindness, hunched shoulders and a small, nodding head. Hands jammed in his pockets, he shoulders open the door of a house and sits down at a table by the window. I can see his legs up on the bench, a pair of misshapen old slippers on his feet and a woman on her knees, cleaning the floor against a backdrop of bottles and frightening-looking sabres.

Only one side of the vegetable cart is painted and the lad minding it is flicking off cockroaches with a wet rag. He has short bleached hair and is wearing a faded blue shirt unbuttoned from top to bottom. The vegetables are lumpy and grooved and the cart's outsize wheels make it look like a tank. The lad sells newspapers too, laid out on a wooden crate, and postcards and old photos under a beach umbrella. Hassan and I admire the clothes and the papier-mâché landscapes and we find it surprising that the faces have changed along with everything else.

Ghosts wander about the courtyard of a mausoleum. Their movements are contorted, like puppets, and they seem to tower over the hedge of spindle trees, the statue and the ladder. Other figures, grey rather than white, are sitting on zinc footstools and keeping up a chorus of throat-clearing and curses. They are discussing the preparations for the next ceremony of commemoration; they say that there's at least one of them a day, they're on edge the whole time. I say this to Hassan; I'm sure it's deliberate, reducing the city to its memories like this, but he thinks I'm talking about the old photos under the umbrella and he laughs.

We leave the river and set off up a steep street, looking down or half-shutting our eyes to keep out the glare reflecting off the walls and windows. It's only just past dawn and already the sun seems directly overhead. I flex my knees as we walk along, and say without anger in my voice, 'This is the last time I go and see an antiquity or a battlefield; places where people have fun – they can be interesting too.'

A man is asleep in front of a car-hire firm, his peaked cap pulled down over his face. There is a din of slamming doors and a shrill voice calling from inside the dark office, but no one answers and the man carries on snoring. Brightly coloured posters are stuck up on the wooden shop front and a woman is wiping her hands on her apron as she calmly observes us. She is sitting on the edge of the pavement between two bowls in which I can see green and brown algae floating.

Hassan talks to me about Firdos where he has friends if I want to have a look around tonight. His delicate gestures complement his descriptions: I picture piazzas lit up like Versailles or Las Vegas and lovers nodding off in bars and those sorts of places. Afterwards you could go for a walk under the arches of the aqueduct and through the trees on the other side of the hill where nothing surprises anyone.

A car crawls past with a loudspeaker on its roof. The

driver scans the passers-by as if he is searching for a friend who he had arranged to meet and the girl talking into the microphone looks thrilled every time she says 'Hello! Hello!' It is one of the municipal publicity vehicles, which announce listings for the different cinemas or sales or deaths. It swerves a little and turns off down a bumpy road lined with unstirring trees.

There are so many images and memories racing through my mind that sometimes I don't know where I am. Sometimes I confuse Hassan with one of my friends as well: it just takes a glance or a word or an affecting mannerism. And plenty of things are not so different from their equivalents in my country: the boys playing soldiers, the windows with wire netting, the stares when a girl passes; it almost makes me feel as if I've gone back to where I grew up. For instance, the man with the pomaded hair lying on the ground by the road looks like Tomi disguised as a beggar, and that old fellow taking it easy in the sun, squatting on his heels, that's another Balao, all ready to tell you his life story – you just have to narrow your eyes until they're almost shut.

When I tell Hassan that I've never thought about my childhood as much as I have done since being in Baghdad, he listens thoughtfully and says, 'Perhaps it has something to do with the transmigration of souls.' He pauses, looks around in every direction and tugs at his braces when he starts talking again. His voice trembles slightly, as if he has a fever. His hair is damp and stuck to his head; he has large rings under his eyes and a black goatee on his slightly sloping chin. He is wearing a short-sleeved shirt, pale cotton trousers and worn-out running shoes. I ask him if he knows Nineveh or Mosul or Fao. Other names occur to him: Hilla, Karbala, Bassorah and Nasiriyah where he was born. He returned there last summer and he was deeply moved seeing the little backstreets again, and the souvenir shops and the caves that date from the Stone Age, but all you can do there at night is go for walks and you end up going to bed exhausted.

Halfway up the hill, in the shade of a balsam tree, a man is repairing a car wheel, his head level with the ground, a cigarette stub tucked behind one ear. He is talking out loud to himself in a voice that sounds assured but still false somehow – perhaps he's imitating someone or putting on an act. Sitting on a stone bench, a boy with bare feet and a bandaged eye looks on, drumming his fingers on a dark-coloured bundle. There's something a bit hammy about him, with his deafening bursts of laughter and constantly nodding head, but look how handsome he is – it's almost magic. Behind him there's an opening in the wall, a staircase with an iron handrail that's covered in leaflets.

We walk between trees marked with red ink and can sense the meanders of a watercourse beneath our feet. There's a sound of knives being sharpened, then an auctioneer's shouts and jingling money: a cattle market. It smells stale, dusty. Hassan tells me that some people come here just to hang about and pass the time. There's not much to see: bales of straw and everybody with their backs turned towards us.

Hassan's eyes are riveted on a patch of open ground bordered by cypresses; we can hear the high-pitched squeals of children playing rib-breaker. We climb the embankment and watch the start of a new game: a little girl, hollow-cheeked with effort, runs between the trees; she dodges some cardboard boxes and throws the ball with all her might but she doesn't hit anybody; the ball bounces down the slope and comes to a halt at the side of a pond where a man without a shirt on is finishing off the contents of a cone of greasy paper. The sun is like a halo above his head when, to more squeals, he sends the ball flying back.

We turn back and come upon silhouettes in high heels, trotting past lowered, garishly coloured shutters. We walk up a flight of steps and push through the pungent smoke of a succession of rotisseries. Two lovers are smooching in the shadow of a doorway and a woman in sandals and a khaki smock is picking up empty bottles with claw-like fingers. She stacks them in a canvas sack, and then sweeps up the dust and cigarette butts from under some formica tables. We leave the spittoons and posters riddled with pinholes behind us, and look back to fix the scene in our memories: the cornices and façades, the street-lamps with their portraits of Saddam, and the people swarming on the embankments like mysterious insects. Below, some lights are still on.

Once we've climbed the hill, we walk along a narrow street lined with buildings painted either pink or white. All sorts of goods are laid out on the pavement: watches, shoes, clothes, trinkets and, outside a pawnbroker's shop, an assortment of rusty keys and locks. The traders sit cross-legged a few feet from the gutter, packed together like stones, lifeless even in the way they fan themselves.

At the entrance to a bare-walled passageway, an old soldier is haggling, a basket tightly clutched in his hand. He gruffly refuses the medicine the woman is holding out to him – perhaps it's out of date or too expensive – so then she looks for others in her bag and pockets.

'It's mostly for migraines,' Hassan says, slapping his forehead. 'They're so bad, you go crazy. Some people choose to die to forget the pain that never lets up; you feel as if your head is going to split in two.' I think of

Saddam again and I wonder if there's a portrait of him
selling medicine somewhere.

Strings of lights are swaying on a row of trees;
Hassan supposes a lorry has just gone past because there
isn't any wind. We walk down the middle of the road
between two cars that have faded in the sun; a man is
standing at the door of a bistro, tugging at his moustache, and another chap, equally sombre-faced, darts
out of a nearby park through a gap in the fence. Glimmers
of sun slip across their backs and the pot-holed road.
At least the children seem more cheerful; they don't
ring doorbells with such ferocity and they can't stop
waving when they see us. A girl crosses the square to
talk to Hassan, while another one hangs back, leaning
against a tree in flower as if she's in a dream; she's
wearing lipstick, has black, curly hair with gold streaks
on top of her head and her eyes are half-closed as she
listens to a Walkman.

The men in front of the music store seem suspended
in mid-air, perhaps because of the steam coming off the
tarmac. We hear boys arguing and threatening one
another and the sound of other, more muffled voices.
Closer to, a couple of men are whistling as they help a
shaky old woman out of her car and accompany her
sway-hipped progress to the door of a shop. A woman
is waiting on the threshold for her with a forced smile

and her eyes in shadow under her hat. Hassan looks towards the park, then the roundabout around which cars spin like tops. This must be just as moving for him as returning to Nasariyah, seeing these huts again, these strips of kitchen gardens and these workmen lying on walls, solving some riddle or other. 'What about Saddam?' I say. 'Doesn't he show himself these days?'

The road comes to an abrupt end at a flimsy painted wooden fence. Hassan climbs over it and signals that we're not far now. We walk past shacks with roofs made of rags, through children who've been running about so much they're gasping for breath. At times they bump into each other and let out a scream and Hassan is amazed they never fall over. I ask him what game they're playing. He tells me about a part of town called Luna Park, where there is a funfair on Sundays with a ghost train and dodgems. I turn my head away, waiting for the dust to settle, and in a doorway, sitting on the step, I see a mother watching. A few clothes hang beside her on hooks.

'Gypsies,' Hassan says. 'They don't travel as much as they used to.'

We walk over piles of rubble, step round twisted girders that stretch their arms to the sky, and stop on the edge of a crater where there's nothing growing. Hassan squats down and talks of the good times: the hookah café near the station, a favourite bar, a cinema, and then suddenly his hands beat the air like wings: a twinkling of an eye and the whole district has vanished. He seems shattered, near to collapse and his earrings dance when he shakes his head; he just can't believe it.

I leave Baghdad with a sense of relief, all that noise was excruciating; several nights I had to get drunk just to get to sleep. I pull over after a few kilometres because the road is so shrouded in smog you can't see more than two feet in front of you, and also because the landscape is changing so fast that it feels as if it's on fast-forward. Uncultivated plains are succeeded by a stony desert where a garrison is stationed, then marshes, fields, grey dunes, expanses of black mud with dredgers at work and lastly crows flocking over ploughed fields.

I drive through hamlets of clay-brick houses hidden in deep hollows, a fortified village as solid as a rock, and a town with a whole district consisting of nothing but rubble, waste ground and cranes rusting over abandoned building sites. The policemen on duty at the crossroads wear torn uniforms and have a week's growth of beard, like in Poisonville.

The traffic crawls along amid a racket of horns and whistles; it's stuffy and the sun's boiling hot. Trucks stop to unload barrels and gas carboys; people sell cooked food on the roadside, along with tyres, petrol in plastic bottles, and wooden and metal wheel-frames. After a bridge I pass kiosks spangled with film posters and a market with stalls covered in cobwebs. Houses are hidden away behind ferns and shop assistants draped in jewellery seem frozen in the doorways of their shops.

I see soldiers more or less everywhere: in open pick-ups parked at the entrance to alleys leading into a square, or leaning against the stone pillars of a building or sitting in the shade of a patched shop awning. A crowd has formed on the pavement in front of a small open-air theatre. It is decorated with garlands and painted signs and on stage a man with sunglasses and a rainbow-coloured hat is holding forth. Around him raised hands brandish flags or wave pennants. 'It's a Bollywood actor,' a woman dressed in her clothes of worship tells me. 'He's talking about his childhood in the shanty towns.'

The houses are low near the dried-up riverbed, the tarmac sticky and there's no sap in the trees. Rubbish is piled everywhere, awnings are falling to pieces and clapped-out cars stand rotting outside hideous build-ings. Hawkers mill about in front of a fire station, whilst vacant-eyed women and a man with a fierce expression wait at a bus stop, stamping their feet with impatience: the heat and smoke and ugliness must really get to them.

Sometimes I don't even notice the people, I'm so lost in my thoughts, wondering whether this trip to Babylon means anything; I can't stop thinking about it. I almost want to turn round and go home but what will I say to my children?

I could tell them about the cows being led out to the fields, the pens of goats and chickens, the orchards and high pastures, the detours I make to look at narrow valleys, canals, dams and mills: about the questions I ask a bare-chested man sitting on the edge of a well who puts his straw hat back on to screen the sun and points out his two sons riding back and forth across the plain on a donkey, chucking stones at birds of prey and stray dogs; about the crying and moaning that comes from all sides and makes my head and my ears feel as if they're going to explode – but I know that wouldn't be enough for them.

I stop for something to eat at Diniyah, a little mountain village veiled in heat haze, and then give Ishmael a lift in front of the mosque that is built entirely of wood, but extended by sculpted columns in the form of arcades. Ishmael wears grey flannel trousers and a short-sleeved shirt buttoned to the neck; he has messy hair and a pallid face dotted with liver spots, but there's a merry glint in his dark eyes and when he chuckles it sounds like he's got hiccups. He is going to Sammara where his brother, his sister-in-law and his two nieces, Rina and Azaida, live.

My mind wanders constantly as he talks to me about steppes, plains and mountains, the Bedouin with their flocks and oases, the ruins of Hatra, and the Tigris and Euphrates, which join at Kurna to become the Shatt al Arab.

'And the people of the marshes who are being forced to move,' he says, staring at a field with short grass which borders the road, 'you know they're wiping them out, just like the Kurds a few years ago.' But he has never been to Baghdad; one day he would like to see its palaces and museums and mosques and Zawra Park, a name known even in Diniyah because of its swimming pool and its planetarium. He sighs, his face suddenly slack, and looks off at the lustrous, sunlit cattle, the stone-walled farms and the village on a hill-side that seems to float in the sweltering air.

We stroll about the streets of Samarra and along the paths that lead up to the palm groves, then we visit the port with its wharves choked with barrels and vast wooden crates. People are sitting out on benches and rocking chairs; there is even a squeaky old swing in a little patch of greenery. We amble along the dock, past a floating landing stage where men in vests are sipping beer and looking at the river, the ships at anchor and some barefooted dockers who are squeezing between the cranes, whistling to themselves.

Ishmael tells his nieces to stay close to the wall; people drive too fast down this street – maybe because it's one way – grazing pedestrians and telling them to go to the Devil. A woman looks at us, lifting a corner of her curtain; her house's shadow stretches towards the shop opposite where a boy wearing a tricorn is hollering to attract passing trade. At moments my eyes close with bliss as I think of my journey, eager for the adventures to come, and at others I'm bowled over by images that otherwise might seem fleeting or anodyne: the engraved stones above the lintels of some of the doors, a man in a striped turban fighting on his own in the grass, workers slumped the length of a wall, a small boat at a bend in a path which a caulker is repairing, tapping his foot on the ground as he works. The street slopes gently down towards a barred fence, which allows one to look into a little wood where clouds of dust are running round a clearing amongst fir trees – children playing football probably. And in the distance a ravine falls sheer away, its sides littered with plastic bottles that glitter in the sun, like a line of revolving lights.

Azaida pretends to be very upset – crying and beating her breast – because she's thirsty; Rina drags her feet so I'll carry her on my shoulders, she doesn't want to do any more walking. We pass a park with a pond in the midst of some scorched grass, a clothes shop, an antique shop, then we enter the shade of a chapel where a woman in a white blouse is selling flowers and a thickly-bearded man is talking, gesticulating with one hand and holding a silver stick over his mouth with the other. I alternate between galloping and hopping as Rina, now astride my shoulders, points out the prison's high walls and a building with narrow passages that rears up in front of us, and then we plunge into a pot-holed street, which is filled with different smells. 'We could have gone a longer way round,' she tells me as we get near her house, and then she would have revealed more of the town's secrets, because everything goes on in the shadows these days. And just as I'm about to drive off, she hands me a pencil case decorated with gold arrows, which she has been hiding behind her back – her father's handiwork and a souvenir of Samarra.

Sometimes at a bend in the road, I glimpse the turret of a tank camouflaged by a cretonne net and I have to go through hundreds of police roadblocks where they ask me all sorts of questions about where I'm from, poring over my name, my country, my religion. They search my bag, my pockets and the boot of the car and they're surprised by how many guides I have. A policeman with a small moustache leafs through them and, turning to his colleagues, shouts that he's got a spy, but it's obvious he's just playing to the gallery or whiling some time away.

The countryside is sad and monotonous after Hamadi. From time to time I see a few goats in wire-fenced pens and flocks of sheep listlessly crossing the ploughed fields. The huts have tyres on their roofs and the few people to be seen on the road are men, mainly old, drowsing on stools, a bottle between their legs.

I look resignedly at my tattered map and wonder if I've gone the wrong way. I park my car in a shaded spot by the river and approach a boy who is hauling himself up onto the bank. He puts on his clothes first, before speaking to me; he has calloused hands and knees, tiny eyes and a face scarred with smallpox. Then he points to a sandy hill and some black rocks. 'It's some-where in the plain.'

I turn my head away as I catch sight of the ramparts, the air is dry and dusty, but you can hear the constant rumble of water flowing in a nearby ditch. I leave the car on the plain in the shade of some wild flowers and start to run up the hill; I want my first sight of Babylon to be from above. But halfway up I have to slow down: the path narrows and then peters out at the base of a lichen-covered rock. I think of Hassan on the edge of his crater as I squat down and gaze at the city that seems to have come straight out of the Bible: it is built like a fortress with tall, tapering spires that whittle away at the sky.

As I walk along, I think about the steep streets of my village and the men in front of their houses or standing in the doorway of a shop. The women and children are already making their way towards church. They cross the field in a straight line and climb the embankment with the slow, resolute gait of penitents. Everyone seems to be wearing their Sunday best – the men in their tight suits, the women slightly stiff in their long dresses and the children in approximations of what their heroes wear, taking measured steps as if they're on a high wire. All that one of them is missing is Zorro's sword and mask – and moustache of course.

I unfold a chair and settle myself under a tree in front of the barracks. Everyone looks down when I catch their eye except for the *halim* seller who greets me as if I were an old card-playing friend. He gives me news of Shakeel, Fatima and Naushad who has left the country and is now a nurse in a home for the disabled somewhere in Arabia. He leans to one side and fixes me with his shining eyes which are so close together he could be a Cyclops, 'How about you?' I tell him I'm trying to forget my village. I almost want to stick my head in the fountain to shake off my torpor and see how beautiful these little brick houses and old men with rust-coloured hair can be. But the moment doesn't last long: a lorry comes thundering down the hill and spoils my view. It flies over the bumps, terrifying the chickens that start flapping about all along the road. 'I know him,' the seller tells me. 'He doesn't even have a licence.' He pauses and I can see beads of sweat stand out on his forehead, and then he adds in a conspiratorial murmur, 'Maybe he's mixed up in smuggling.'

The stench of fat and burning rubber has seeped into my skin and clothes; at first I just thought that there was a bad smell wherever you went. Black smoke from roasting chickens forms a sort of vault above the rotisseries and the air is filled with fine dust, bits of straw and tiny flies that are dazzled by the sun. Their buzzing makes the heat even more stifling and I wonder if you swallow some every time you open your mouth. I mop the back of my neck with my handkerchief and look at the street sign, then at the crowd of cripples on the square. They are holding flowers that jump and dance in front of them in a blur of shapes and colours.

That's the first tie I've seen in Baghdad, I think,

as I watch a man step off the bridge that spans the ravine and nimbly steer a path between the potholes in the street. He has a bag slung over his shoulder and a hat with feathers in it which he wears low over his eyes. Craning his head forward, he looks across the street at the entrance to the mosque; half-asleep children are filing in, one by one. He wipes his feet on a threadbare doormat and pushes open a swing door. He reappears, bald now and much thinner, in a narrow room where two waitresses are walking between the tables. There is a picture hanging on the wall; it shows wild animals and Saddam in a hide felling them with blows of his club.

Hassan was right: you could find your way about Baghdad just by portraits of Saddam. In Haifa Street, for example, under the neon sign saying *Bonnie and Clyde*, he is sitting on an upturned boat and, I suppose, looking out to sea; there's a blue glint in his eye and patches of sun dappling his cheeks. He is wearing a white boater with a green ribbon, a shirt open to reveal a hairy chest and a camera is dangling on his stomach. He is on holiday, probably at Fao where he has several palaces. It's strange, you find the same portrait under the railway bridge, except that in that one he has sunglasses and a machine gun instead of the camera. And in front of the red-brick prison, it must be in Port Said Street, what's he meant to be there – a cosmonaut or a blow-up doll? Anyway, near my hotel he's selling fennel-scented water.

The arcades are full of kids selling trinkets and medicines, shining shoes and handing out leaflets. I turn the corner and skirt the rubble of a devastated street. In front, bent double under the weight of her basket of provisions, a woman is singing; her voice carries a long way. We barely seem to get anywhere, despite our pumping arms and legs; the street climbs steeply in the full glare of the sun. She is called Mirna; she is going to see her son Khalil who lives on the right, almost at the top of the hill. We see empty sacks spread on the ground and part of a garage with a shingle roof; a giant vetiver hedge hides the house itself. She closes the garden gate behind her, hunchbacked no longer, and starts singing again.

A man is sitting on the edge of a ditch, staring anxiously at the sun. Another is leaning against a low wall that bounds a pen; his eyes dart over a patch of waste ground where children are playing and a wheel-barrow is sliding backwards. Both of them are wearing firemen's helmets and workmen's blue overalls. The one who looks like Turko the Terrible finally straightens up and stubs out his cigarette with trembling fingers.

Slowly gazing around, I take in the whole district. I recognise the sycamores and the gables that slant shadows across the fronts of houses. There are other kinds of trees, and tall coloured street-lamps and windows with small panes and unbleached canvas curtains. I go up to a boy in a white skullcap; he's sitting on a stone in the brilliant sunshine leafing through a magazine, but he does not know the name of the street. He calls his sister who gestures evasively as she answers, 'Mansor.' Then she pads away, her body hidden by a colourful trellis, her head lowered as she crosses the passage to the glass door of her house.

All the walls have messages and watchwords on them that overlap in a tangle of swirling letters. *Holy war*, they read, *Vengeance. Moorhen. Go and see Ziyad. Boxing match at six at the skull and crossbones pavilion.* A man in shirt-tails cuts across a building site towards a clump of reeds while some labourers sieve sand, dancing around like Redskins. Behind them, on the far slope of the valley, one can see white cabbage patches, mountains of watermelon and a scarecrow with ten arms standing in a field of narcissi. I stop near an abandoned sentry box and take a map out of my pocket. I look for Mansor and Palestine streets and using the scale, work out the distance between them.

These are also the first rickshaws I've seen, although they actually look more like handcarts; one is pulled by a man with a sombre, fearful face, whereas another fellow waves his hat very heartily and his medals flash so brightly in the sun, they make your eyes hurt. The cart moseys along, wending its way through the dust to a makeshift bar.

I glance round the moustaches and then up at the troop of girls stretching their necks out in front of them as they climb the hill. My physical appearance, and perhaps my clothes too, give them hysterics. Silver bracelets slide up and down their arms as they push back their hair, which is still wet; there is a river below. I can hear whistles calling and answering, conches and good-humoured, slightly tipsy singing.

On one side of the road a solitary, cracked building with two watchtowers like two big obelisks stands marooned in a desolate expanse. Rows of slate slabs jut out of the dry, powdery soil around it; it must be a cemetery. On the other side of the road, a boy with a crew-cut is sitting on the front bumper of an old car, which he is repairing and insulting at the same time. Dogs are sniffing the tyres, wheel rims and doors in silence. Suddenly, to their left, a man appears out of the grass, dragging a ball that looks as if it's solid lead. The dogs start howling and circling him and the car horns go crazy. A rusty object hits the ground with a metallic clang and the dogs immediately retreat behind a mound of stones. The boy hands his shawl to the man, retrieves his plug spanner and goes back to his bumper, bathed in sweat.

I walk past open doors, heads floating between curtains like lotuses and walls splattered with flecks of spit. I lean my elbows on the wall and watch the beggars in rags on the bank and a child who is strolling along, running his hand over each of the trees that bend down to the water. Street hawkers eat in the shade of their stalls, staring at their reflections, and a woman adjusts her stockings as she looks at the picture of a Russian circus on an old poster.

I set off again, remembering the first photo I saw of Babylon; it was in an old dictionary. I shut myself in my room and spent a long time studying the ruins divested of their layers of earth and the black stones laid flat, in a line; that was when I promised one day to see the scale of the whole plain. Other photos followed: reconstructions of avenues, the Ishtar Gate, towers, the walls of Nebuchadnezzar's palace – it looked like a set on Cinecitta. When the war started, shells and rockets and fireballs began raining down in my mind, but I didn't tell anybody; I kept it all to myself as I shed that skin and separated myself from my childhood.

A car guns its motor and trundles away, breaking my train of thought. It goes around a bend and disappears into a side-street behind a restaurant with picture windows and enormous fans on the ceiling. Leaning his back against the bar, a man is playing an instrument that looks like a dulcimer. Beyond the restaurant there's a shoe shop, a domestic appliance shop at the foot of a flight of steps, an ice-cream maker's delivery tricycle and a house with shutters that fold back like an accordion. Then there's a school with a faded façade and a yard choked with wild grasses that's like a little wood. The people say they're too poor to be able to pay teachers, so their children hang around the streets and play catch with stones. And the streets are filthy; they must look like pools of paraffin when it rains, with all our leftovers floating about.

The children made a racket this morning. They were pretending to be a derailed train, or a bomb, whistling and roaring and massacring songs by the dozen. I saw them as I came out of the hotel and asked them if they'd teach me to sing or to whistle; they just stood there looking at me, gesturing with their feet, their noses running. Their parents were drinking, sitting on wooden crates or squatting on the bare ground of an old battle-field. One of them got up to ask me for a cigarette; he had a bottle sticking out of his romper-suit. Same as everywhere else, there were some of those emaciated kids who play football on the embankment or sit round drumming on barrels.

The bar owner looks like Hassan in a pirate costume. The haircut and the round doll's eyes are the same, even if one eye is coloured glass, which sparkles. He breathes shallowly and asks me if I'm drinking in, because otherwise there's a thirty dinar deposit. I lift the door curtain and sit on the end of a stone bench next to a pair of twins. Both of them are intently watching a tanker going upriver; they have beards and are wearing the same kind of black hat. From here one can see a mass of scrap metal and blurry patches that slowly shift position, like the hubbub in the back room. Suddenly the two men get to their feet, walk through a clump of reeds and in turn become two dark patches on the sunlit riverbank.

One can also see the Hayder Khan mosque; the houses are low at the front and the view of the terrace particularly open. Ochre and sulphur buildings form a sort of high wall behind the mosque, above which the sky is constantly changing colour: violet, scarlet, jagged gashes of white, patches of silver dust and bands of vermilion that grow thicker in the distance. As for greenery, all that's to be seen are bulbous date trees, scattered in clumps like mirages.

Two children are shouting insults and thumping one another as they pound down the steps in a thunder of hurrying feet. Bed Wetter is wearing khaki shorts and an embroidered shirt with a sash round his neck; Pig-Headed has an oval face, pale, furtive eyes and a hollow-sounding voice. They must have a bit of a fever; they're shivering as they whack each other with their plastic rackets, then they step into the street and carry on muttering threats at a zebra crossing. They look like a ventriloquist and his dummy.

I cheer myself up by thinking about my village and the names people have there: Cayman, Cardigan, Rusty because he's got fishy little teeth which he never brushes. As for Black Box, he spends his days listening to the radio for news of the team he's supported since he was ten, and he never stops talking about them. Anything will do: where the new stadium's got to, or what's happened to Malarai who you never see these days. At night he hangs around on the beach or, when it rains, with the squatters. And he's always the last to get off the streets: they are his African fastnesses.

I set off up a lane without a name, or any shade, that's lined with wood and brick houses with verandas out the front and bare gardens. Under the boiling sun, it climbs to an esplanade and a flat park that stretches into the distance. Boys are chatting in low voices in front of a building with a collapsed roof and they look me in the eye as I approach the old, low wall that's in ruins. They're talking about the Russian circus's tour, which is being shown again on television; no one can get enough of seeing the lion tamer's head in the beast's mouth. Smells of frying and black smoke float between the boys and the building and catch in my throat. I step off the pavement and wave my hand a few times over my head to shoo away the flies.

A hose-pipe is draped over a shrub; white clothes are drying behind the wire mesh of open windows and the bamboo blinds are all down. A young girl is picking over lentils or rice on her balcony; she is wrapped in a prayer shawl and stretches periodically out of boredom or tiredness. And once again there are children dressed in blue with caps with stars on them, perhaps it's the insignia of their tribe. They're watching the water running in the gutter and toads jumping in with splashes that throw up arcs of water like the folds of a fan.

I carry on my way past ripped posters, a shop with flaking paintwork and dead hedges with great gashes in them. Nylon shopping bags, floor cloths, tiny, white-fenced pens, columns and black rocks – these are what you see most. The pavements creak slightly and the bus shelters are almost toppling over backwards. I notice long dark veils, some scruffy boys in a side street and other, even skinnier, ones who are kicking up dust around a kiosk.

Further on, at the corner of a gravel path, I ask two

men what they are playing. The one sipping his drink seems to be examining every card in the pack in turn; there's no end to it, he says so himself, and adds that he can spend days without thinking of anything except rummy. A dog bumps into a streetlamp trying to get out of my way, which makes the man in striped trousers laugh; he calls out to me in a kid's voice, while the other one reaches for his hat. The dog limps off between some dustbins, barking at a bus that lurches into motion with a sharp jolt. A car horn blares and a woman with brown teeth, having just turned into the lane, checks herself and heads calmly towards a car packed with soldiers who look like they're going into a trance.

I can hear a reedy voice and footsteps on paving stones: a woman is crossing the park in the shade of the trees that stand out against a low sky. Constantly shaking her head, she searches through the bushes and scruti-nises the branches of the trees; she has curly hair, big wrinkled eyes and a mouth that twitches uncontrollably, but her voice as it calls again is the only thing that seems real. I lounge around with the slouchers on the riverbank, then go and lean against a pockmarked brick wall to have something to eat and watch the bamboo rafts that are scraping against a flimsy canoe.

'It's too hot to breathe,' complains a man who is wearing matching tracksuit bottoms and polo shirt. He spreads a mat on the grass, takes off his sandals and hands me a bottle of a gold-coloured drink. He tells me about Baghdad in winter when at that time of day fires suddenly start appearing everywhere, except in the parks, of course, and in the woods which then become very dark. I look up as I hear the tinkling of a little bell and see mules and a Moses basket that have been left on the stone steps. 'Has that woman lost someone?' I ask. He taps his temple with his index finger, 'Her mind. That's what she's lost.'

I stop for a minute to look at some people working on the quay. A lad is rolling barrels from a boat to a red lorry, passing under a mounted statue of Saddam who is trotting towards the disused lighthouse. In the foreground, to the left of the statue, stands a floating crane where black-beaked birds are spreading their wings.

A buzz of voices rises up from the river: a woman takes off her grey cloth cap and scratches her head as she examines the cables which a giant of a man and some other workers are unrolling. And that child with the skin drawn tight over his bones, he must be the water carrier; he walks down the wooden gangway, bucket in hand, knocking over any crates in his way. A man calls to him in a quavering voice that seems to resonate a long way; he is working in the sun on a boat which looks as if it's made of cardboard and string, and he's thirsty.

A taxi cruises along the pavement, its radio playing

softly. The driver has a shaved head and a bushy black moustache. I hear a train whistle behind the buildings on the avenue that have been bleached by the sun. At a set of traffic lights, a girl is selling wire necklaces made with a knife. Her eyes are a luminous grey and she has yellow smeared around her mouth. I lean against the fence of a warehouse and try to take in the whole avenue. The people look as if they're out for a leisurely stroll, with sparrows following their every step: perhaps they are on their way home from the embankment and couldn't be happier with their walk.

There's a queue in front of the cinema. It must be a love story; the poster has a half-naked man and woman, but also an old man perched on a ladder who's observing them with a scowl on his face: the girl's father, prob-ably, furious at seeing his daughter with such a poor man. It's often like that in Indian films, and then it turns out the man has a fortune and everything ends up sorting itself out. The bar next door is full of teenagers with motorbike helmets under their arms. The boys have shaved heads like the taxi driver and the girls black plaits tied up with coloured ribbons.

I ask a tin-plate seller if he knows Luna Park. He flicks a cloth at the wall of his shop, which is abuzz with flies, and then walks out with me to the crossroads. Craning his neck, he points out a street lined with dead trees.

'It's not difficult. You take that street and just walk along the stinking canal, then you turn right after the hospital and left before the building with red and white flags and that's Palestine Street.'

The street has ditches on either side, which, in places, have been filled with polished stones. The paint-work on the walls of the houses is blistering and behind the windows, silhouettes bustle about, watching the passers-by. A woman is carrying a child in her arms and talking to it about what she can see around her – a parched field, some holly bushes and other children who are throwing stones at a rusty rubbish bin.

I pick my way through the assortment of bricks, planks and cardboard boxes on the pavement, past people drinking in open-air bars and dogs waiting by the tables, mesmerised by their own shadows. You can hear the orchestra from here: a few furious riffs and the singer's clear voice that conjures up the lonely plains, like cotton fields when no one's working in them any more. And then, there, the cymbals come in, sounding like they're being smashed to pieces.

This part of town resembles a labyrinth, perhaps because of the tangle of paths winding between the houses. Hoarse cries echo from a hollow in a patch of waste ground, shouts and laughter loud enough to decap-itate the devil. A young girl lowers her eyes when I go up to her; she has patches of eczema on her forehead and rings in her nose and bellybutton. I look at some paper animals on the edge of a pavement, the threadbare clothes hung on clothes lines and the tired face of a woman who calls me, rubbing her hands together, 'Come here sweetheart, we won't be bored.' The pimp blows his nose noisily, flexing his knees in front of a canvas tent with two exits.

And then here it is – Luna Park. It's written in bold letters on billboards. I stop by a wall and empty my mind; I want the funfair to absorb me completely. A gladiator comes towards me, covered in gold, gesticulating with his sword and net, followed by a man dressed in flannel pyjamas and a boy in a vest who is carrying a radio on his shoulder. We look at each other like people who recognise each other. I listen to their footsteps and the rats squealing under the paving stones. Suddenly the din of wheels of fortune is deafening and when they catch, they throw off coloured sparks, and that gypsy playing darts and dancing at the same time, that's amazing.

There's such a crush in the alleys that you're liable to get a whack if you don't pay attention to the people who barge past you or step on your toes without saying sorry; otherwise they stare you in the face or scrutinise your clothes; they know you're not from here. They always ask me the same question, 'Is this your first visit to Iraq?' and then they want me to talk about my country, which steadfastly remains a mystery to them, despite my lyrical evocations of the cane fields. As a last resort, I draw two circles in the air, a big one next to a small one, and I tell them it's near Madagascar. At which they either laugh heartily or look blank: they've never heard of Madagascar either.

I go through a ceremonial gate in the shape of a pyramid and see a delivery-man laden with knick-knacks near a stall. A child shuffles sideways, his head swollen with hydrocephalus. My neighbour's son suffers from the same illness but he doesn't run around, he prefers to sit in the sun; his mother tells him off the whole time because it gives him spots on his back and face. I look at the scene painted on a wall of a bar: a woman is lying in a wheat field; she is wearing a patterned dress and there are flowers and Christmas bells falling from the sky. I lean my elbows on the counter and order a beer from the waitress with red hair gathered in a bun at her neck. At the back, in shadow, a man is counting money. He is wearing a sequined suit and brown leather mules. Sitting on the opposite corner of the table, a cat observes him, its lips working as if it is eating.

Someone asks me if I can move over a little; he has red eyes and a curling moustache that is almost white under his nose. He explains he needs the space for his belly and his wrestler's arms. He leans against the bar and a little smile appears at the corner of his mouth; he was just talking to his wife this morning about starting running again. Do I know Sandow who? I should go and find somewhere more peaceful to sit, maybe in the alley where the police are patrolling. He puts his hands on my knees; I was about to get up anyway, and I lift them off to go and have a look at the stalls and the gallery and the ceremonial gate. People are rushing past in a sort of stampede. He mutters a few words; he has a voice that conjures up the danger of being trampled under-foot, that advocates not getting sucked in but waiting quietly until the crowd has stopped flooding past.

'She's pretty, the girl playing darts,' I say.

He watches her until her turn comes to an end and she goes and sits down on a bench among some other gypsies.

'She's pretty,' he says in a quiet voice, and then searches through his pockets; he pretends to be thinking about something when he takes out a knife. 'Do you want to fuck a gypsy?' he asks, and with a quick motion of both his hands he shows me the district they live in, Cheikh Marouf, on the other bank. 'If anyone causes you trouble, just ask for Cassidy, everyone knows me over there.'

'What about the Cheikh himself,' I ask as the noise of conversation resumes, 'do you like him?'

He must have heard something else because he starts talking about power cuts at night and goat-herds who play the pipes – it's like a Pessoa poem. He puts his knife back in his pocket and walks away on tiptoe, alongside a fence covered in lichen. After a few paces he turns round to see if I'm in danger.

The orchestra strikes up again. I hover around some chairs that have been set out in a corner and cast my eyes over the stage where a few couples in fancy dress are dancing. Everyone is talking at once and Scheherazade has to shout to make herself heard by the king who squeezes her buttocks: the music is too loud. I do an about-turn and walk past merry-go-rounds with wooden horses, dodgem cars and flying carpets. The operator of the last ride gives me a little tap on the back: 'It's easy,' he says, 'you just sit on these cushion things and then they start jumping all over the place when you least expect it. It's best to hold onto both reins, otherwise you go flying, like a rodeo.'

Children seem to fall off a lot, perhaps on purpose, and when the ride stops they crawl out from between the cushions, looking around them with stunned expressions on their faces; flames and cloven-hoofed devils are painted on the partitions between the cushions.

I sit down on a bench next to a peddler with a long beard. He sniffs the cake he's holding before eating it. Then, to drum rolls, the tombola's winning tickets and matching prizes are announced. 'They're shutting,' the peddler tells me, shaking his clothes; crumbs fall on the gravel and are immediately hidden by clouds of midges. The alleys are almost empty, but the stage is crowded with people gawping at the musicians as they pack away their instruments. Further on, workers are taking down the booths and waitresses are picking up armfuls of cups. A lorry loaded with crates of beer groans on the paved square as cars purr at the main gate.

The street bends and draws closer to the river as it climbs a hill. It is flanked with grimy buildings, sewers and a clump of trees amongst which children as raw-boned as greyhounds are running about. Men are sitting on piles of bricks, drinking *arak* or with their mouths full of fish bones. I stride resolutely across the square and start up the street. Leaning her arms on a windowsill, a young woman is watching night coming down the hillside. The first lights of evening are moving along the road and the sky has turned a seaweed green.

I don't see them until the last moment; a bunch of teenagers standing to attention block my path at the entrance to an arcade and call me 'Major', or 'General, Sir'. I look at them to see what I can tell from their eyes or their clothes, and I hear the peaceful rustle of trees and footsteps echoing in the courtyard of an old wooden building. One of them, with red hair, grins from ear to ear as he scratches his temple with his pistol; he must be the clown of the bunch. Staying on my guard, I glance furtively over my shoulder: what's Cassidy up to?

The swarthy one talks to me in a calm voice, repeating things or rephrasing them, he's keen to explain the exact situation: they have no work, they haven't a penny for food and as for any sort of entertainment, the thought never even crosses their minds; they haven't been to a film or out dancing for years. Life is not such a bed of violets, or roses, so they scrounge off their friends; it's only a loan, after all. He raises his hands apologetically and searches my pockets, a process which lasts long enough for them to list all the countries they'd like to go to: the names sound like an incantation. Then he hands my wallet to the clown who leaves me five dinars for a taxi.

A man spits at some pigs that are frisking about in the bushes alongside the dyke and on the other side of the low wall a goat has been tethered to the frame of a half-built pirogue. I hear breaking glass, footsteps, banging saucepans and see bars and crowded pavements and patches of light on people's faces. And look, here comes the army: a hairy fellow with a scar, that extends his moustache, and two one-armed friends who must have seen their fare share of wars; their medals are all different colours and shapes. A child is with them; he's wearing a marine's beret and he groans, nodding and saluting when he sees me.

I stop in the middle of a grey stone bridge and look along the embankment from end to end as I imagine my return to my village. In my mind's eye I can see a barely paved street that smells of incense; it's lined with one-room houses and dilapidated shops where friends drink and smoke until they start hallucinating, a state which they've given a name, based on the noises you hear in your head; bong and bang, I think.

I love the thought of telling them about my trip but I also wonder what I can say that will captivate them. I think about Babylon and its visitors, who seemed to me as beautiful as its ruins, and the silence and the dusty green plain for miles around, and then about Baghdad and its medicine sellers and the statues of Saddam everywhere, even in the cemeteries. I'll tell them how noisy the city is, the constant racket. Digging, drilling, hammering on every street corner, car horns blaring for no reason, guns going off, and when people talk to each other it's as if they've got a microphone in their stomachs. Even the music on the radio sounds like rats running around a kitchen. And I'll add, 'Just like the village'; that will make them laugh.

We walk side by side in silence. This is my last night in Baghdad; tomorrow I'm going over the desert to Amman. I can picture the charred cars abandoned by smugglers at the frontier and the high-tension cables, which serve no purpose now except than to mark out the road. The driver puts the music on full blast so as not to fall asleep: the journey is a monotonous straight line. Luckily there are sorts of mirages that enter one's mind; one can see fires on the dunes, men and camels coupling in huge blue canvas tents.

As I turn over these memories, I realise we've gone round in a circle. I recognise that old gentleman leaning against the pillar and the weirdly hooked knob of the walking stick propped at his side. He's chewing on a cigarette and absent-mindedly watching some children who are hopping about on the esplanade. Painted wooden caravans are drawn up along the canal; they must be for tonight. Women are sitting on a mattress on the ground and a man on crutches is limping between some bushes, his every movement shattered into fragments.

When I tell Salma that there's almost too much to see, she stops for a moment by the fence of a maize field. It's hard making out her face, the road isn't that well lit, but I can tell she's looking at me wide-eyed as she murmurs, 'Another time.' She takes my hand, plays with my fingers, then suddenly cuddles up to me like a child, her arms round my neck. I think of the desert again and a thousand little things that I immediately forget, but the feeling of leaving remains, overwhelming me afresh.

We can see other fields and a few scattered houses painted white with blue shutters and a shed that looks like a fairground booth. A paraffin lamp is hanging at its door, feebly illuminating some vine-clad arbours and patterning the occupants' faces with rings of light and inky shade. All the men have gold teeth and their eyes seem to roll like madmen's. Salma tugs my arm and asks if I'm scared; it must be a thieves' den. Her expression changes when she sees a striped hammock at the back of the shed and a photograph of a baby hanging on one of the varnished wooden walls.

A light moves down the steps and casts the shadow of a thin silhouette with a battered old headdress on the crumbling walls. The figure cracks her fingers and

neck and brushes past a child who is raking the gravel.
She switches off her pocket torch and launches into her
tirade with an amused laugh; she seems from another
world. Then she opens the slatted door and slips out
into the moving crowd. It's dark again under the trees
and not a breath of wind stirs the leaves.

Salma turns the corner by the wooden building and
looks at the people in the street. Two women are sitting
on the ground, their backs against the roller door of a
warehouse. They are talking nineteen to the dozen,
fanning themselves with bits of cardboard. Two lovers
are leaning on a fence with their arms around each other:
a young girl in a party dress and a boy in a t-shirt and
jeans with pockets on the knees. They are looking at a
long, brightly coloured queue stretching towards a
cinema ticket office. Hovering in front of a bistro, his
legs trembling, a grey-haired colossus of a man is singing
in a deep voice. He's wearing new boots, a suit with
gold buttons and a cowboy hat perched on the back of
his head. Salma balances herself on the edge of the
pavement and tells me about the people in Baghdad
who think they're in a film and get all their gestures
and expressions from actors; it's their way of looking at
life through rose-coloured spectacles. 'Or maybe it's
because they like stories,' I say.

Some children run out into the road, as if they're

lost, babbling away in caustic, shrill voices and letting out harrowing screams that burst my eardrums. They have a wooden mask, a green painted stick and an umbrella, which they are trying to frighten each other with, and they tear off down the slope, screaming even louder. There's a squealing of tyres as a lorry comes out of a bend and brakes viciously to avoid the smallest of the children. The driver curses Ratface who runs to his mother who is calling him loudly. His cheeks are covered with red blotches and his dark eyes seem to shine with a demented joy.

Salma pushes open the door of the bistro and glances around at the piles of suitcases and canvas bags, the puffy, sleepy faces lined with wrinkles and cracks, the open trunk full of provisions, and the hats, glasses and bottles, full and empty, on every table. Steadying himself on a walking stick, a man quickens his step and goes to speak to a woman in uniform who is holding tightly onto a wall. Her expression becomes distant and she seems to answer with a hint of regret. Beyond them the pillars are blue stone and the floor is covered with greasy bits of paper. And in a corner of the restaurant, between two tubs of sand dotted with cigarette butts and plastic cups, a child is alone with its marbles and a dog is lying on its back, gazing up at the lights and the insects playing with their shadows.

We sit at the bar near a group of teenagers and order a beer, a house cocktail and some vegetable fritters. Old framed photos on the wall show overjoyed railway workers standing in front of a steam train, a station master waving his little grey flag and sycamores along the avenue as tall as the station buildings.

'The Karbala train is late,' the barman tells us in a lazy voice. He jerks his chin at the occupied tables with their places set too close.

Near the emergency exit a hawker is trying to sell cheap shoes to three silhouettes in black. We can hear sums being mentioned, outraged responses, talk of losses and money to be recouped and then a girl butts in, interrupting the hawker with an abrupt motion of her hand. She is wearing a yellow dress and would like various different pairs of high-heeled shoes.

Salma crumbles a fritter and tells me that she has always dreamed of driving across Iraq, stopping wherever she wanted. I ask her if there are places she'd like to visit and she tells me about Najaf, the city of gravediggers, Fao, the ghost city and Bassorah on the Shatt al Arab with its marshes and reed palaces, because it's a terrible waste not knowing your own country.

'How about you,' she says, twisting round on her stool, 'how was Babylon?' I put my tankard down on the bar and shake my head: I have almost completely forgotten, but it will come back later, or else I find it difficult to talk about. She doesn't insist, but brushes her hair off her forehead and looks at an old woman who is begging in silence, squatting in a striped loin-cloth.

We hear gunshots when we get outside. Dogs begin barking and running in all directions and bats leave their branches and fly in circles over our heads. A woman picks up a screaming child and walks back and forth across the garden, from one bench to the other, fanning the child with a handkerchief. I peer at a dark path along which men are walking in nightshirts. The trees seem to have been turned to stone; there's not a breath of wind and in the distance one can see the light of the street-lamps falling like sheets of rain on the passers-by and the flags.

'Someone's calling you,' I say, stopping by a wooden pole. Salma stands on tiptoe and stares at the passengers of a stationary bus. A man has stood up, taken a few steps on the broken paving stones and now he calls her again from the opposite pavement. He is wearing baggy trousers that are frayed at the bottom and a luminous flowery shirt.

'My neighbour,' she says, raising her arms in a victory salute. 'He looks like a singer but I have forgotten his name.' He goes and sits back down on his bench near a canal in which flowerbeds are reflected, while she beats time, drumming her fingers on the parapet. One of her knees is jiggling under her dress and she looks from the man to the pole. 'Yes, you're the same.'

We talk about the people who are being displaced or fleeing the country. Most end up in makeshift camps, packed in like rotten fish. Salma has an uncle in Iran and cousins in Amman. She'd have liked to go too, but her parents had no money. She kicks a tin can furiously, sending it skidding down the bank; anyway, she couldn't live anywhere except Baghdad. We hurry past a bushy hedge and watch children going to their homes in a dark little alley. There's a lot of laughing that goes on and on and whistling and merry, mocking calls.

'Sticks and dirt,' she says, referring to the court-yard of a white-washed building. The pediment is cracked and the vegetable garden overgrown with weeds.

A man appears at a turn in the road, bent double in the dust as he strains to pull a cart. He's like some-thing projected by a magic lantern: you can't hear his footsteps or the cart's wheels; there's only two sets of shadows going up the street in strange silence. They lengthen as they cross the bridge, and then disappear behind the railings of a garden in full flower.

'A smuggler,' Salma tells me. She slows down in front of a shop window and distractedly reads the adverts.

Suddenly her face becomes gloomy and lines appear around her mouth. 'They're hand in glove with the police. Not that that stops them blowing each other's brains out now and then when resentments build up.'

We can see the church's reflection in the shop window; its courtyard is full of cars and dogs strolling along by the wall. On a table by its gate, a hunchback is unwinding crepe streamers and a strip of printed material that looks like parchment. He rolls his eyes when he sees a child on all fours in piles of dead leaves and roughly gestures at him to go inside. A man takes off his hat as he passes under the porch and goes through the spring door that is framed by crowns of thorns. He falls on his knees in front of the altar rail and seems to stare at the brown cotton ribbon hanging above the pulpit between two garlands of marigolds from the marshes.

It's the heat that's driving people out-of-doors. Lovers walk under the trees of the avenue, a man with frizzy hair on his chest is sitting on a little ruined wall, taking the air, and a girl in high heels is click-clicking merrily along by a building's front door. It's the heat, the migraines and those bombs no one can forget. A glass door opens at the end of a passage with a slightly vaulted ceiling that is lit by the weak, misty glow of a lamp. A woman in a brightly coloured dress leans on the door and calls in a childlike voice to an old man who is drowsing on a venerable divan. He mops his forehead under his broad-brimmed hat and yawns unceremoniously as he contemplates the crows flapping their wings in the trees.

'I've never been to Babylon,' Salma says, her eyes turned on a narrow path, which winds through an overgrown garden and then perhaps down to the river. But she remembers photos in her school books and Nebuchadnezzar who she used to think was a horse like Pegasus. She smiles and leads me to the bottom of the garden. She stays silent for a moment, lying on the grass near the rock; a delivery tricycle spins on the spot, tyres squealing, then rides off amongst the flowerbeds with a jingling of little bells.

'The river air will do us good,' I say, passing a building with a clock with figures on it and casement windows. We squeeze between billboards to get to the wall which we lean our elbows on as we watch a ship docking. Men covered in medals like admirals gather on a part of the bridge that is lit by multi-coloured lights. We can't hear what they are saying but it must be important; their eyes bulge as they talk and they wave their arms about as if they're looking for buoys to grab hold of. Some raise their heads: a voice from a loudspeaker announces that the anchor has been dropped, they can disembark.

'An argument,' Salma says to me when they start trading blows. 'It's too hot.' She rubs her face with the sleeve of her dress, as if she's wiping off the grime.

'How do you say "sun" in your country?'

'We say "sun".'

Her lips part in a vague smile as her unblinking eyes remain fixed on the mêlée. A few passers-by stop; some heads even appear at the windows of a building facing onto the dock. I put my hand on her shoulder and whisper in her ear, 'But we call streetlamps "first lights".'